The Keeper of Her
HEART

The Keeper of Her
HEART

USA TODAY BESTSELLING AUTHOR
STACY HENRIE

Copyright © 2021 Stacy Henrie
Print edition
All rights reserved

No part of this book may be reproduced in any form whatsoever without prior written permission of the publisher, except in the case of brief passages embodied in critical reviews and articles. This novel is a work of fiction. The characters, names, incidents, places, and dialog are products of the author's imagination and are not to be construed as real.

Interior Design by Cora Johnson
Edited by Joanne Lui and Lisa Shepherd
Cover design by Stacy Henrie and Rachael Anderson
Cover Image Credit: Arcangel. Photographer: Joanna Czogala

Published by Mirror Press, LLC
ISBN: 978-1-952611-08-7

AMERICAN HEIRESS SERIES
Night at the Opera
Beneath an Italian Sky
Among Sand and Sunrise

LOVE INSPIRED HISTORICAL
A Cowboy of Convenience
The Rancher's Temporary Engagement
The Outlaw's Secret
The Renegade's Redemption
Lady Outlaw
The Express Rider's Lady

OF LOVE AND WAR SERIES
Hope at Dawn
Hope Rising
A Hope Remembered
A Christmas Hope

Prologue

Yorkshire, April 1908

"IT'S NOT PROPER, Ada. And I will not abide it any longer." Charles Thorne's voice could likely be heard belowstairs by the Stonefield Hall servants. "You will give up riding out alone, or I will sell that horse of yours."

Ada kept her hands clasped demurely in her lap to hide their trembling. It wasn't fear she felt—it was anger and confusion. "I don't understand, Papa. I have always been allowed to ride Prince Albert alone on the estate."

"What your father is trying to say," Victoria Thorne interjected in a more subdued tone, "is that next week, you will turn sixteen, darling. The year after that, you will be out in society. And it is no longer ladylike to ride about without a proper chaperone."

Charles bobbed his head in agreement, but his dark eyes were still as stormy as Ada knew hers must be. After all, the two of them were cut from the same stubborn cloth.

"I shall have one of the stable hands accompany me, then."

Her father threw his hands in the air and stalked to one of the drawing room windows. "You're not thinking as a young lady ought. Riding about in the company of the servants is nearly as unseemly as riding out alone." Crossing his hands behind his back, he turned to face her again. "You are reaching an age when independence of spirit ceases to be a virtue. If it ever was . . ." he added in a mutter. "Perhaps we have indulged you too much in the way you spend your time."

The first prickle of alarm crept up Ada's spine. She loved the freedom of her days—reading, riding, walking about the estate or to Gran's house. What would she be expected to do once she turned "of age"?

Her mother supplied the dreaded answer. "It's time to begin your training in earnest, so you are well prepared before your next birthday."

"My training?" Ada repeated past her closing throat. "Training for what?"

Charles let out an immense sigh as he glanced at his wife. "In spite of all the well-qualified governesses we've employed for her, we have surely failed."

"Tis not true, my dear. Ada has a very keen mind and a lovely complexion. We have not met with failure yet."

It was not the first time her parents had discussed her as if she were not present. But today, after hearing the bitter news that her daily rides alone had come to an end, their detached discussion only added to Ada's mounting frustration and the headache building behind her eyes.

"What is it I am to be trained for?"

Her father shot her an impatient look. "To be the wife of a gentleman and a proper society woman."

"Once I fall in love," she added.

"Pardon me?" He eyed her in confusion.

Ada sat up straighter. "The training is to help me be a

wife and a woman in society once I've fallen in love and married."

"Nonsense," he countered. "What does falling in love have to do with marriage?"

Shocked by the strange question, Ada looked to her mother for help. But Victoria's expression appeared pained as she returned her focus to her stitch work.

"You do wish for me to love the man I marry?" Ada's heart thumped faster with sudden dread.

"We want you happily settled." Her mother directed the words to her needle and thread. "Love does not have to come in the beginning, Ada. If a couple is well-suited and equally matched in station, they may discover a type of love throughout their marriage. Certainly, they can expect a fondness to grow for one another."

Ada let her mouth drop open in unladylike astonishment, though no sound came out. Didn't her parents love each other? Was that not the reason they had married? Pressing her lips together, she studied them carefully. They seemed to share the sort of fondness her mother had spoken of, yet Ada had never sensed a deep connection or affection between them.

And clearly, they expected her to follow a similar path.

Desperation strangled her breath, making her light-headed. "If I do not marry for love, then what is the purpose for such a union?"

"To maintain the life you have always known," Charles said, his voice rising again. "You will marry a man of good breeding and fortune who will see that you want for nothing."

An image of a pampered lap dog came to Ada's mind. No wonder she preferred horses and their strength and power to other creatures meant to sit lovely and silent.

"Do you understand what we are asking, Ada?" This time, her father's tone was softer, more placating.

Rising to her feet, she nodded. "I will not ride out alone anymore, and I will become the well-bred young woman you wish me to be." She purposely left off the final item, regarding marriage, from her list of commitments.

"Very good." Charles looked relieved. "You may go on up to bed now."

She kissed her mother, then bid both her parents good night. But as Ada rushed up the stairs, eager to escape to her room, she felt a heady rush of determination. She would keep her word about the riding and her training, but she would never settle for a marriage without love—never.

No matter how rich or poor or well-bred the men who came to court her, she would marry for love, or she would not marry at all.

Part 1

Chapter 1

Yorkshire, April 1910

IN THE LIGHT from the single lamp, Ada Thorne eyed the open wardrobe and its remaining contents. Most of the gowns, including the plum dress of silk faille that she'd put on, wouldn't exactly suit her future role as Ned Henley's wife.

"I believe that's all the dresses I shall need," she whispered to her lady's maid, Hetty Trumble. Ada's trunk sat open beside the bed, already half-filled with clothes, undergarments, books, and a few pieces of her glass jewelry. Her real jewels were in a bank box in London and not likely to be accessible without her mother or father present. And after tonight, it would surely be a long time before either one spoke to her again.

Her maid was kneeling before the trunk, helping Ada pack, her face ashen in the dim light. "Where will you live, miss?" she asked in a worried tone.

"For the next three weeks, I'll be living in Scotland."

"All alone?"

Ada shook her head, though she couldn't share any more

information with Hetty. There was too great a risk of her parents learning of her whereabouts before she and Ned were officially married.

"Why Scotland, miss?"

"Because unfortunately, even at the age of eighteen, I'm not allowed to marry who I wish without my parents' permission. However, in Scotland, I can," she said, smiling, "providing I've lived there for twenty-one days."

"Ah, very clever, miss."

Ada searched the room for anything else she might wish to bring with her. She'd lived her entire life at Stonefield Hall. It felt strange and surreal to think of leaving it, let alone living elsewhere.

"After we are married, we will be moving to London." She added some of her childhood books to the stack inside the trunk. "Mr. Whittington has promised to help Mr. Henley find a position there."

Hetty glanced at her. "Which Mr. Whittington, miss?"

"The elder son, Hugh," Ada answered absently, gazing about at the familiar furnishings and knickknacks.

Would she ever return home? She didn't know. Not if her father had his say. He'd made his thoughts quite clear last night. If Ada went ahead with her plans to marry a gamekeeper, she would not be welcomed back at Stonefield—ever again.

"Ah. The more serious of the two Whittington sons," her maid said, "but I say he's the handsomer."

Ada didn't respond. Hugh Whittington might be serious and attractive, but it was Ned, with his kind blue eyes and handsome face, who'd been a beacon to her, a steadiness in the otherwise glittering but cold world of the upper class.

After talking to him during a shooting party last year, Ada had made certain her daily walks took her in the young man's vicinity. They'd courted secretly for the past six months before she'd announced to her parents that she and Ned intended to marry. Yet she'd known nearly from the first moment they'd met that she was in love with him.

"You won't ... starve ... in London, will you, miss?" Hetty shut the trunk lid and climbed to her feet.

Forcing a light laugh, Ada slipped her coat on over her gown. "No, I don't believe we shall starve."

Deep down, though, a germ of fear attempted to sprout inside her. She'd never known deprivation or difficulty or hard work. But she was determined to see her decision through—she would prove that marrying for love wasn't the swift path to misery and regret that her parents believed it to be. She loved Ned. And she trusted that his current employer, Hugh Whittington, would follow through on his promise to assist Ned in finding new work.

A move to London would hopefully bring them more opportunities and independence. At the very least, it would put needed distance between Ada and her parents and the way she'd been brought up. She would raise her family differently. Her sons and daughters would be encouraged to marry for love and to lead lives of compassion and goodness rather than ones motivated by appearances, position, and wealth.

"We shall be fine, Hetty," she said as she quieted her momentary panic. "Now help me carry this trunk downstairs." She didn't wish to wake their butler. He would surely alert her parents of her departure, and Ada wanted to be long gone before they rang for their breakfast in a few hours.

Even with the trunk only half-full, it wasn't light. Ada gripped one of the side handles and her maid the other, and together, they lugged it out the door. Moonlight from the large window on the landing lit their path down the carpeted stairway to the front door.

As they exited the house, cool air rushed up the stone steps and across Ada's flushed cheeks. Shadows obscured the gravel drive, but she thought she could see the outline of a wagon a short distance away. Ned had come for her as they'd planned.

"A little farther," she coaxed Hetty. The two of them hauled the trunk toward the waiting vehicle.

"Ada," Ned called out quietly.

She directed her maid to lower the trunk to the ground, then Ada rushed forward to embrace Ned. His tender kiss to her cheek abolished any remaining doubts or fear.

She was following her heart, and like Ned, exemplifying a bit of faith in the process. Whether that was in herself, in them, or in God, she still couldn't say. But she did feel content and free, and that was something she hadn't felt in a very long time.

Once Ned had secured the trunk in the back of the wagon, he nodded toward the seat. "Ready, love?"

"Nearly." Ada turned to face her maid. "Thank you for all of your help, Hetty. Please see that my mother and father receive my farewell note." In it, she'd written that she was happy and hoped, eventually, they could be happy for her as well.

Even in the faint light, she caught sight of the girl's curtsy. "Yes, miss."

"I shall miss you." In a sudden wash of affection, and possible homesickness, Ada embraced her maid. "I wish I could take you with me; truly, I do." But there was no extra money for employing the girl—now or in London. Ada stepped back. "My mother will surely find a new position for you here at Stonefield, but even if you leave, I am confident you will not want for a position. Not with your talents and proficiency."

Hetty sniffled as she bobbed her head. "Thank you, miss."

"We should go, Ada." Ned slipped his hand into hers and gave it a squeeze.

She cast one long glance at the shadowed manor house before turning to face her husband-to-be. "I'm ready now."

Though she suspected she was dreaming, Ada felt certain if she placed her hand alongside the oak tree's trunk that the bark would grate against her palm. She knew at once where she was—after all, she'd stood in this exact spot numerous times, waiting for Ned.

Anticipation blossomed in her stomach as she turned away from Stonefield's oldest tree to face the nearby Whittington estate. Rainy mist shrouded the details of the neighboring property, though the splaying branches of the tree kept her protected from the elements. Any minute now, Ned would materialize through the fog to meet her.

But he didn't come. The tendrils of fog thickened, obscuring Ada's view in all directions. Her excitement soured into concern, then alarm. Where was Ned? Had he forgotten all about her? She tried to swallow past the panic coating her throat to call out his name, but the mist choked her . . .

Scrambling to sit up, Ada placed a hand against her nightgown, where her heart still thudded with fear. Moonlight doused the room through the open curtains. She wasn't at home beneath the old oak. She was in Scotland, and had been for two weeks, in the home of one of Hugh Whittington's sisters and her husband.

Ada lay back down and pushed out a breath. There was

only a week to go before she would travel by train to meet Ned for the wedding. A keen longing to see him filled her with an almost physical ache. They'd exchanged letters, but it wasn't the same. She wished to see his face and the love she felt for him reflected in his blue eyes and quick smile.

Was she secretly worried Ned had changed his mind about marrying her during their prolonged separation? Could that be the reason for her dream?

She wasn't sure she'd blame him if he *had* decided against the wedding. Ada had detailed in her letters how she'd been assisting the great house's cook and housekeeper to learn the skills she would need in her new life. But perhaps that had been an unwise idea.

It was painfully obvious from her fumbled attempts at cooking and cleaning that she had no hidden talent for housekeeping. She felt as if she was living the reversal of a fairy tale, in which the princess had become the servant instead of the other way around. Still, Hugh's sister and her husband had treated her kindly, even if they weren't quite sure what to make of her domestic lessons.

"Despite that, Ned still loves me," Ada whispered into the darkness. "He loves me."

There were other things she'd felt less certain about, such as where they would live in London. Ned had secured a position at a print shop, but they did not yet have a flat. The uncertainty about their housing had also wound its way into Ada's dreams, at least until she'd received Ned's last letter.

I promise we won't be in the slums, he'd written. That reassurance alone had brought a relieving chuckle to Ada's lips and an eventual end to the nightmares of living in a one-room tenement crowded with other families. *We'll find us something, Ada. I have every faith we will. I love you, my darling. And that love has only grown these past few weeks.*

Recalling his words once more, Ada felt her heartbeat finally slow to normal. She had faith in Ned. He would be at their wedding next week and with her all the days after that. She would cling to that reminder and repeat it as often as she must until she was in his arms again.

Ned removed his worn cap from his curly brown hair as he followed the Whittingtons' butler into the study. If he were heir to an estate—he grinned at the unlikely possibility—he'd have a study that looked just like Hugh Whittington's.

The desk and bookcases were made of rich, warm wood, and the chairs were comfortable. Ned liked the paintings especially. One showed a restless group of hounds and horses before a fox hunt, while the eager riders sat proudly in their saddles. The other painting showed their return—the weariness of the animals and the triumph of the hunters in their mud-spattered clothes, their catch in hand.

"Mr. Henley, sir," the butler announced.

Hugh stood up from behind his desk. "Henley, good to see you again."

"You, too, sir." He shook Hugh's hand.

"No need for formalities. Call me Whittington, please." He motioned for Ned to sit, then Hugh did the same. "Especially given that as of today, you no longer work for the estate."

A fact that still felt as strange as it did right. Ned's father and grandfather had both worked as gamekeepers for Whitmore House. He had followed in their steps, certain he would live and die in the same cottage the Henleys had occupied for decades.

That is, until he'd spoken with Ada for the first time.

He'd been aware of her existence for some years, since the Thornes' estate neighbored the Whittingtons', and the two wealthy families often did things together. But when Ned had seen her at one of the shoots last year, he'd realized she was no longer a girl. She was a beautiful, confident young woman of seventeen.

He wasn't the only bachelor—rich or poor—who'd noticed Ada that day, either. However, to his surprise, she'd hung back from the others to ask *him* questions. Ned found her smile and clever sense of humor charming, though he had no expectation of seeing her again after the shoot. He was astonished when Ada sought him out the next day, and the next. They began meeting regularly beneath the old oak on the Stonefield Estate.

Ned didn't like keeping their meetings a secret. He wished he could visit with Ada openly, without concern for what the other servants or her parents might say or do. The two of them weren't doing anything wrong. But secret or not, it wasn't long before he couldn't imagine not seeing and speaking with Ada every day. Soon, their conversations included talk of a future together. He'd taken the matter to the Lord in prayer and had felt peace about asking Ada to marry him. And she had accepted without a moment's hesitation.

Did she still feel that way? Ned shifted in the chair, his gaze on his tattered cap. It wouldn't be the last thing he owned that was a bit shabby. In contrast, Ada had grown up with new things and nearly endless wealth.

Her letters from Scotland had amused him with tales of her newfound housekeeping skills and had endeared her to him all the more. But would she survive a life in London? Would the independence and opportunity they sought in the city eventually strip the vitality and youthfulness from the woman he adored? If so, he would have only himself to blame.

"When is the wedding?" Hugh asked, thankfully pulling Ned from his gloomy thoughts.

He lifted his chin. The smile he wore was only a bit forced. "Day after tomorrow. I—*we*—can't thank you enough . . . Whittington. For writing to your sister, for helping me secure a new position." Ned cleared his throat. "I hope you hold no ill will toward me for leaving. I believe the new gamekeeper'll do well."

"I harbor no ill will." Hugh's earnest tone matched his expression. "On the contrary, I rather envy you, Henley."

Ned couldn't help a startled chuckle. "Truly?"

"You have the opportunity to try your hand at something new, something your fathers haven't already labored over for years." The man's gaze moved toward the window. "I don't know that I would have the courage to make a fresh start in that way."

His words surprised Ned. The Whittingtons, like the Thornes, weren't titled, but a successful boot factory had helped the family amass a sizeable fortune. Hugh had taken over the management of both the factory and the estate at the age of twenty, when his father had died. But perhaps there'd been other things the young man had wished to do.

"What would you do if you could start over?" Ned asked, only a bit chagrinned at his boldness.

Glancing back at him, Hugh drummed his fingers on the desk. He didn't seem offended by the question, to Ned's relief. "Perhaps that's the trouble," he said after a moment. "I am not at all sure what I would do." He smiled ruefully. "My sisters have each set their course with their husbands, and Harry has always exhibited a passion for the military. Whereas, I, on the other hand, knew I would inherit the factory someday, and so that is what I learned and focused on since I was a boy."

Ned could relate in a way—he'd been raised to take over

for his father, too. And though he liked books and working with his hands, he hadn't expected to do much with either, except to continue caring for the game animals and the forests surrounding the estate.

Yet to have a man like Hugh Whittington feel envious of him—now that was something unfamiliar.

"Enough about that," Hugh said, straightening. "I asked you here so that I might give you your final wages and share some additional news I hope will be welcome to you and Ada."

Nodding, Ned tried to hide his surprise once more. He'd been expecting his wages, but nothing more.

"An acquaintance of mine has been heavily involved in a housing project near the Thames for the past nine years. He and others like him were eager to provide more suitable housing for working-class men and their families." Hugh folded his hands on top of the desk and leaned forward. "I wrote to him a few weeks ago, inquiring if there were vacancies in any of the houses or flats, and I received his reply yesterday."

Ned could guess what the man's answer was by the enthusiasm on Hugh's face, but he still felt the need to ask, "What did he have to say?"

For weeks now, Ned had been praying to find a respectable place for him and Ada to live. But he hadn't been able to shake his concern at finding a place that was decent *and* affordable.

"I'm pleased to report there is a vacancy in one of the flats," Hugh said with a smile. "Unfortunately, it only has three rooms."

Ned hurried to swallow a laugh when he realized Hugh believed that might be a problem. "That's brilliant. Thank you, Whittington. It's most kind of you to ask for us."

"My pleasure." He stood and picked up an envelope from

off the desk. "The name of my friend and the address of the flat are inside. If you wish to rent the place, you may let him know by telegram. There is a bit extra in there as well, beyond your wages, to help with the first month's rent, wherever you choose to live."

Rising to his feet, Ned hoped to convey gratitude, even as he refused the extra money. "I appreciate that, more than I can say. But I can't accept. I earned what I earned and not a penny more."

"Your integrity and hard work are worth a few extra pounds, Henley." Hugh extended the envelope toward him. "Please, consider it a wedding gift."

Ned hesitated a moment longer, then took the envelope, knowing Hugh wasn't likely to be persuaded otherwise. "Thank you again, for everything."

"I'm grateful to be of assistance." He stuck out his hand, which Ned shook a second time. "You and Ada will be missed, but I wish you both all the best in your marriage and in London."

Setting his cap on his head, Ned smiled. "We wish you the very best, too."

He felt as if some of the weight pressing down on his shoulders the last few weeks had lifted as he saw himself out and headed down the drive for the last time. Ada would have a decent home in London. As far as the rest, he would trust in God and in his and Ada's love to see them through.

CHAPTER 2

STARING OUT THE train window at the greenery passing by, Ada tapped her right shoe beneath her long skirt. She released the tension in her gloved fingers, then clasped them together again to keep them still. Only a few minutes more, and she would arrive at the station where Ned and his mother would be waiting for her. She already felt as if she'd been riding the train across Scotland for days instead of two hours.

She couldn't wait to be reunited with Ned. At the thought, her stomach filled with eager flutters. Three weeks was far too long to be apart from each other.

The train began to slow. In contrast, Ada's heart threaded faster. This was it. All that stood between her and Ned was less than a quarter of a mile of track.

As the railway station came into view, she scooted closer to the window to see if she could see him waiting, that ready grin on his handsome face. There were more people about than she'd expected, and Ada couldn't see him right off.

Once the train jolted to a stop, she grabbed her purse and stood, relieved she had no other luggage to manage in her hurry to disembark. Her trunk would be unloaded for her.

Ada moved briskly down the aisle to the door of the train car. A worker assisted her down the short flight of steps. The instant her shoes hit the ground, she surged forward into the milling crowd.

She wound her way toward the station benches, doing her best to be polite even in her eagerness. However, neither Ned nor his mother was among those seated outside. Ada slipped into the station building next, but she found no familiar faces there, either. Her enthusiasm began to bleed into concern.

"He'll be here," she murmured to herself as she retraced her steps outdoors. But the reassurance fell flat.

Was Ned simply late? Or had he changed his mind . . . The flurries in Ada's middle stiffened and became sinuous vines, curling and knotting tighter and tighter.

She forced herself to think rationally. She would see about her trunk. The plan eased a little of the tension inside her, but not so much that she could breathe easily. She located a porter and was relieved to find that at least her trunk had ended up in the right place.

"Where are you, Ned?" Ada whispered to herself as she paced beside her trunk, her purse handle choked between her hands. Now that she'd found her luggage, she didn't wish to leave it. Surely, Ned would guess that she'd be waiting for him beside her trunk.

The train she'd arrived on was preparing to leave now. A number of the station's waiting throng had already climbed aboard. Those who had disembarked when Ada had were nearly all gone as well.

She tried to swallow past the surge of fear that pooled in her throat. What would she do if Ned failed to show? Should she return to Hugh's sister's house? Or go home and beg forgiveness from her parents?

Ada's mouth pulled tight at the latter thought. No, even if Ned had changed his mind about her, she would not go back to Stonefield Hall. If she did, she would never be able to live life on her own terms and fulfill her own dreams.

Perhaps she could find employment for herself in London. She could live in the flat she and Ned had planned to rent. But oh, how empty and lonely the place would be without Ned at her side.

Ada's attention was drawn to a man rushing alongside the train as it began to slowly roll forward. She couldn't see his profile since he faced the train windows. Yet after a moment, she recognized his long gait and the cap on his head. Her anxiety became elation at once.

"Ned!" she cried out, not caring if she drew attention to herself. Rising on tiptoe, she called his name again as she waved.

He stopped abruptly and wheeled in her direction. When he saw her, his entire being seemed to sag with immense relief. All except his smile, which shone brighter than Ada had ever seen it.

In several long strides, Ned reached her and crushed her to him in a fierce hug. She wrapped her arms around his waist, pressing her cheek to his jacket and relishing the reality of him. She never wanted to let go.

"Our train was late. And when I didn't see you . . ." He eased back just far enough to place a firm kiss on her lips that melted her fears.

How could she have doubted? His love for her was as real and deep as hers for him.

She wasn't the only one sacrificing for this marriage, either. Ned had given up a position he excelled at and loved to try something new, so that Ada and their future children might have a home filled with far more than tangible things.

"I never want to be away from you again." She placed her hand alongside his jaw.

His familiar laugh washed over her with all the sweetness of coming home. "Can't tell you how happy I am to hear that, love. I was worried you'd changed your mind."

"I worried that perhaps you had," Ada said with a chuckle that was possible now that she was no longer gripped with fear.

"Never." After a glance at the nearly empty station, Ned snuck another kiss. "I say it's well past time we're married, Ada Thorne."

"So do I."

The wedding took place in an old Scottish church that reminded Ada of the one in the parish back home. She wore the evening gown she'd brought with her from Stonefield Hall. It was a cream-colored silk charmeuse, which succeeded in highlighting her dark hair and eyes. Ned's mother, Maud, had helped her dress that morning and surprised Ada with a small bouquet of flowers to hold.

Ada and Ned had both tried persuading his mother to join them in London, but the older woman didn't wish to live away from the family cottage or her husband's grave. Maud reassured them that she'd be fine, though Ned insisted on continuing to give her some of his earnings to add to the stipend the Whittingtons were already paying her.

Ada scarcely heard a word the priest spoke. She was too consumed by conflicting emotions. Marrying Ned was what she wanted to do. However, her father's predictions that she would end up penniless, haggard, and miserable repeated through her head and stoked nervousness within her in spite of her jubilation at becoming Ned's wife.

Somehow, she managed to voice her vows at the appropriate time. Then Ned was leaning forward, her hands still cradled in his, and kissing her tenderly. The ceremony was over. When her husband stepped back, his gaze searched hers. Ada could read the question in his blue eyes as clearly as if he'd spoken it aloud.

Did she regret her decision?

"I love you, Ned," she murmured. Bestowing a kiss to his lips this time, she didn't care that it might be viewed as too bold. She needed to reassure him—and herself—that they were doing the right thing.

Ned squeezed her hand. "I love you, Ada Henley."

"Mmm." She smiled fully. "I quite like the sound of that."

He laughed as he led her to where his mother sat waiting. "You look lovely, dear," Maud said as she stood and embraced Ada. "I doubt there's a more beautiful bride in all of Scotland."

"Thank you, Mrs. Henley."

The woman's heartfelt compliment brought tears swimming in Ada's eyes. They were as much from happiness as grief. Growing up, she'd always imagined her parents and her grandmother in attendance at her wedding, hugging and congratulating her. Their absence today, while expected, still made her heart ache with longing.

At least her grandmother hadn't condemned her for her choice to marry Ned. Lucille Devon had replied to both the letters Ada had sent to her from Scotland.

I will not pretend to understand what you are doing, Ada, she'd written. *But I hope you will continue to write me regularly. I could not bear losing touch with my granddaughter.*

"Ready for our delicious wedding dinner?" Ned asked.

In truth, they would be eating another meal at the inn

where they were staying. The teasing question succeeded in pulling Ada's thoughts to the present. She linked her arm through his, grateful and amazed to know they were truly married now. One look at his warm smile soothed her grief. There may be those who were not here with them, but she would not let that spoil this joyous day.

Four days later

Wrapping her arm around Ned, Ada pressed her cheek to the back of his nightshirt. She didn't think she'd ever tire of the sense of security she felt lying close beside him.

"Can't sleep, love?" he murmured. His fingers twined with hers where they rested against his chest.

She shut her tired eyes. "No."

Tomorrow, they would leave Scotland, and their short honeymoon, for London. Ada wondered for the umpteenth time what awaited them there. The possible answers brought a mixture of excitement and trepidation that kept sleep at bay.

There was still so much that was unknown. She'd never been to London, and Ned had only been once for his interview at the printing shop. Most of her life, Ada had believed her first trip to the city would be for her debut season. Yet she felt no loss at trading lavish gowns and social events for a humble life and modest abode with the man she loved.

"I can't settle my thoughts," she admitted, opening her eyes.

"About?"

"London, the flat, your position at the printer's."

Ned shifted and rolled onto his side to face her, wide

awake now. "I'll care for you, Ada." His low voice rang with conviction. "Same as I promised you and God at our wedding."

Ada knew very little about God—to her, He'd always been a distant figure with little interest in the lives of those on earth—but she knew Ned. And he was a man of his word.

"I trust you." She cupped his jaw with her hand as a swell of love overwhelmed her.

His eyes appeared more black than blue in the half-light of the room. "I can't promise a life of ease, like the one you left behind."

"Which suits me perfectly well," she said with firmness. "I want a home full of love and hope and laughter—all those things which cannot be bought with money."

She thought she saw his mouth lift in a smile. "In just a three-room flat?"

"Yes." She chuckled at their private joke, born from Hugh Whittington's apology regarding the size of the flat. "Besides, I believe cramped quarters may prove to be of greater advantage than sprawling manor houses."

Ned laughed heartily at her remark before she covered his mouth with her hand.

"You'll wake the guests next door," she protested, though she couldn't hold back a smile of her own. She loved making Ned laugh or laughing in turn at something he'd said.

"Very well. What is to be gained from a cramped flat?"

Ada burrowed into the crook of his arm. "Well, to begin, it is far more convenient to simply roll over and tell you when I cannot sleep than to patter barefoot through a series of rooms in order to reach you."

"Ah." She heard the unmistakable amusement in his voice. "If only the upper class knew what they're missing by owning so many extra rooms."

Poking him in the ribs, she incited another deep but muted laugh from him. "That's not the only reason. I have seen far more of you these past six days than I ever did while living at Stonefield Hall."

"Afraid that might have more to do with us being married now, love." He lifted her hand to kiss her fingertips, sending shoots of feeling tripping up her arm beneath her sleeve. "You don't have to wait by the tree 'til I'm done with gamekeeping, and I haven't started work at the shop yet. So we've had ourselves all day . . ." He placed a kiss on the end of her nose. "And all night to be together." He tilted her chin upward and captured her lips with his.

After a minute or so, Ada eased back to trace his jawline with her finger. "Do you think this position at the printer's will be a good one?"

"I believe so," Ned said with a nod. "It should keep us in the flat and decent food on the table."

"Then all shall be well."

She sensed his earlier somber mood settling over him again, even before he encircled her in his arms and spoke. "It won't be easy, Ada." The gravity had returned to his tone. "We can manage, though, can't we?" His question in that moment was not so different from his silent one on their wedding day.

"We can and we will," she said with more than manufactured confidence. When she kissed him, it was much longer this time.

However unpredictable or difficult their life in London might prove to be, Ada would not complain. She would never give Ned cause to doubt her resolve.

Chapter 3

LAUGHING, ADA CLUNG to Ned's neck as he carried her up the stairs and across the threshold of their first-floor flat. She'd been pleased, and more than a little relieved, to see their building was one in a tidy line, with brick exteriors and slate roofs.

"What do you think, love?" Ned set her gently on her feet. "We've our own bath scullery." Removing his cap, he used it to point toward the partially open door ahead of them.

With a nod, she moved down the short hallway and into the living area. While spartan in appearance, the flat was clean and boasted of electric lighting as well as a range and boiler. The cook at Hugh's sister's house would likely approve of the contraption. Through the other two doorways, Ada saw what would be their bedroom and parlor.

"It's perfect, Ned." She returned to his side to kiss him.

His expression held tangible relief, but also mild concern. "Even without much furniture?" They'd been informed there was a bed frame and mattress in the bedroom, and a table already sat in the center of the kitchen area, but nothing else.

"Yes," Ada answered.

She walked to the window that overlooked the back of the building. A narrow staircase led to a small garden. Perhaps there might even be room for her to plant some vegetables if she could figure out how. If only she'd consulted more of the servants, such as the gardener, for helpful hints before she'd left Stonefield.

Ned wrapped his hands around her shoulders and pulled her back to lean against him. "Once I've been working at the printer's for a bit, we'll purchase us some chairs and a sofa."

"We'll be fine until then." She rested her hand over his.

He twisted her to face him. "It's rather humble, but I believe we'll be happy here, Ada. You and I . . ." Pressing his forehead to hers, he grinned. "As well as those little ones who come along."

Her cheeks warmed with a blush, yet she couldn't help smiling at the thought of having their own family. She kissed Ned soundly to show her agreement, her pulse racing.

"I'd best see about our trunks," he said after a long moment, his tone laced with regret.

"Go on."

Ada unpinned her hat and used it to fan her face as she walked over to the range. Thank goodness she'd learned how to cook on a similar mechanism in Scotland.

What would her parents think of the simple flat and her new responsibilities?

Her laugh sounded as merry as it did brittle in the empty room. "What's begun is begun," she firmly told the four plain walls. "And I would not change a thing."

Deep down, she hoped Charles and Victoria Thorne had softened their opinion of her marriage to Ned in the four weeks since Ada had been gone from Stonefield Hall. She wanted to teach her children different values than the ones she'd been taught, but she longed to do so with her parents' blessing. Surely, they could still correspond with her, as her grandmother had been doing, even if they didn't condone her decision.

The sound of footfalls came from the hallway. Moments later, Ned and the two men he'd hired to help them entered the flat's main room with their trunks in tow.

"If you'd be so kind as to set them both there," Ada instructed, pointing near the table.

Once the trunks were in place, Ned paid the two men a thruppence each, then shut the door to the flat, cocooning them in their private world once more.

"Did you read that letter from your gran yet?" he asked as he rested his cap on top of one of the trunks.

In the excitement of traveling and her disquiet about what sort of condition they'd find the flat and the neighborhood, Ada hadn't remembered the letter in her pocket. "I completely forgot." Ada removed the letter. "Do you mind if I read it now?"

"Not at all."

Placing her own hat on the table, Ada took a seat on the other trunk, partially facing the window. "See, we have no need for chairs," she joked as she tore open the envelope.

Chuckling, Ned slid the first trunk toward the bedroom.

Her grandmother talked about the weather and about an evening party at Stonefield the week before. But Ada found herself skimming the trivial news, anxious for some word about her parents. Had they come around?

I miss you dearly, Ada, as do your parents, I am certain. However, I regret to say things have not changed on that front. Your father is still adamant we act as if you are no longer with us, though I know it breaks my daughter's heart to acquiesce.

Please keep me apprised of your life in London. I truly

meant what I said in my other letter. I wish you and Ned much happiness.

The sincerity of her grandmother's words did little to quell the piercing ache that rose inside her. *My parents are choosing to act as though I have died.* Ada lowered the letter to her lap, where several tears splashed against the page.

"What did your gran have to say?" Ned asked from behind.

Ada jumped to her feet, her back to him, and hurried to remove the evidence of her tears before he caught sight of them. She wouldn't have Ned thinking they were tears of regret.

"She's well. And what's more"—Ada spun around, pasting on a bright smile—"she wishes us happiness here in London."

Ned studied her a moment before dipping his head in a nod. "That's good of her. And your parents?"

"They have not yet come around," she said briskly as she knelt to open the trunk. "But I'm certain they will."

If he heard the errant hollowness in her remark, he didn't comment—and she was grateful for it. She would not let her parents' continued stubbornness mar this day of new beginnings. However, as she moved about unpacking, she felt the hurt of her grief burrow deep within her heart.

After seeing Ned off for his first day at the printer's, Ada tidied up from breakfast. She'd never washed a single dish before going to Scotland, but the task no longer eluded her. Cooking, on the other hand, was still a challenge. She and Ned had prepared supper together the night before, using the food they'd purchased yesterday to stock the cupboard as well as some meat and vegetables from a nearby market. But today, she would be on her own to make the meals.

An unfamiliar sense of loneliness wound through her as she stood in her dressing robe, surveying the flat. She'd never wanted for company when she required it. Yet here, she had no family or friends or beloved horses to occupy her days. Only Ned, who would be gone until supper.

"Still . . ." Ada folded her arms against the feeling of isolation. "There is plenty enough to occupy me until Ned's return."

She changed into a moderate day dress of sea green with appliquéd flowers at the high waistline. It was a rather extravagant gown for housework and cooking, but it was the most basic of her dresses. Perhaps in another month or two, she might be able to afford more sensible clothes.

Tying on the apron the cook in Scotland had gifted her, Ada decided her first order of business would be to see what she could do to clean the old mattress she and Ned were sleeping on. She had a vague memory of the maids back home whacking the rugs and mattresses with sticks several times a year to rid them of dust and dirt.

She stripped the bed of blankets and dragged the mattress through the flat to the back steps. The mattress was heavier than she'd anticipated for being rather thin, and Ada was breathing hard by the time she wrestled the object down the stairs and into the garden.

Trying to catch her breath, she sucked in a gulp of morning air—and nearly choked. The fog was dissipating, but the smells of the river and the city remained behind, heavy and pungent. And the noise. She'd been surprised by its loud cacophony last night as she and Ned had walked to the market. This morning was no different. Even here, surrounded by tenement buildings on both sides, she could still hear the clatter of wheels, the clop of horse hooves, the hum of motorized vehicles, and the rise and fall of human voices.

Ada searched the ground for something to strike against the mattress. When she didn't find anything, she returned inside to grab one of the fire pokers.

Her first thwack produced a plume of dust that made her eyes water and her nose itch. Sneezing, she struck the mattress again. The repetitive smacking soon tired out the unused muscles in her arms, but she was determined to have a clean surface to sleep on.

Once she finished with the first side, Ada awkwardly rolled the mattress over and whacked the other side. Overall, she thought the thing looked slightly cleaner, but she wondered if she was only imagining it.

Getting the bed back inside proved more difficult than bringing it out had been. Sweat had formed beneath her collar by the time Ada slid the mattress back on the bed frame.

She opened every window in the flat after that to make use of the breeze, malodorous or not, then she remade the bed. It was another skill she'd never had to learn until recently. With that done, she decided the floors could use a good scrubbing.

Three moderate-sized rooms and a scullery didn't seem like an excessive amount of floorboards to wash, but her back and knees ached before Ada had even finished the parlor. Tendrils of her hair stuck to her damp forehead, and her soaked hem made her dress heavier. What seemed like hours later, she finally dumped the last of the dirty water from the bucket outside.

She felt a sudden kinship and compassion for the maids and footmen at Stonefield Hall as she sank onto the trunk beside the table and kneaded her sore back. How did they endure this sort of work day after day without complaint? Would she be able to endure it, or would she be running to the nearest train station by the end of the week?

Shutting her eyes, Ada forced a calming breath. There was nothing waiting for her back home, unless she showed up alone. And she wouldn't do that. She could do this—for herself, for Ned, and for their future family. Self-pity was not a path she would allow herself to traverse.

She ate a cold dinner, in an effort to rebuild her strength to prepare supper. She very much wanted a warm, delicious meal ready for Ned when he arrived home.

Following the Scottish cook's written recipe, Ada chopped, mixed, and prepared six meat pies and placed them in their mold. Then she stepped back to study her handiwork. The tops of the pies looked a bit over-handled, with the crust thin in some places and thick in others. Still, she was proud of the general result. They were the first meat pies she'd made entirely on her own, without someone instructing her over her shoulder.

She carefully slid the mold into the range. The cook had given no specific length of baking time—she'd told Ada more than once that the look of things determined if something was finished or not.

Ada decided she would give the pies ten minutes or so before checking on them. She collected one of her books from the parlor and sat on the trunk to read. However, her eyes kept falling shut.

"I'll only sleep ... a few ... minutes," she murmured, resting her head on her arms.

A burnt smell nudged her awake sometime later. She sat up and blinked in confusion. Was there a fire outside? The scent didn't seem to be coming from the open window, though. As her tired mind became more alert, she suddenly recalled the pies.

"Oh, no! No, no, no!"

She leapt up and threw open the range door. Heat and smoke billowed into her face. Ada hurried to bat it away. Had she ruined the pies completely? She grabbed the mold with her apron, but the fabric wasn't thick enough to block the heat from reaching her fingers. With a yelp of pain, she dropped the pies onto the clean floor.

Her fingers began to smart, along with her eyes from the tears she refused to release. Ada dampened a corner of her apron and held it against her hand as she sank onto the trunk again.

"What an absolute mess I've made of things."

She shook her head at the three burnt spheres that had managed to tumble free of the mold. The others looked too scalded to slip loose. There would be no delicious meal for Ned now. Sharp disappointment cut through her, more painful than the receding sting in her fingers. She'd wanted so much to prove to her husband, especially on this first day by herself, that she could manage this kind of life. But if she couldn't even make a proper meal . . .

The tug to give into tears of defeat nearly overwhelmed her. Until Ada remembered her father's arrogant predictions for her life. She might have limited control over becoming penniless or haggard, but she could choose whether to be miserable or not.

Determined once more, she rose to her feet. "I refuse to choose misery over scorched pies." Regret and frustration, perhaps, but not misery.

Ada placed the runaway pies back into the mold and set it on top of the range. Then she used a rag to wipe up the burnt flecks from the floor. She didn't have enough ingredients to begin again without going to the market for more, so that was where she would go. Ned might have to wait for his supper, but he would have it nonetheless.

She changed into a different dress—one that wasn't damp and didn't smell of smoke and sweat. Once she'd rearranged her hair into a fresh knot, she pinned on her hat. Ada locked the door of the flat behind her and set off in the direction of the market.

The constant movement of people, horse-drawn vehicles, buses, and motor cars was vastly different from the relative quiet and slower pace of the countryside. Yet Ada didn't find the contrast unappealing. There was an energy in London— the thrumming of the past and present—that swept everyone along in its wake.

After only one wrong turn, she located the market. As she handed over her coins in exchange for the meat and then the vegetables, a peculiar worry, one she'd never experienced before, wound through her. Was she being wasteful by purchasing more food? Would Ned find such an action extravagant? Ada hoped not. She was committed to providing him a proper meal and not a burnt mess.

The activity in the streets had increased during the short time she'd been at the market as workmen began returning to their homes. Not that Ada felt fear being here by herself. There were other women and lots of children about and plenty of daylight remaining. As she walked, she found herself watching those around her, wondering what their lives were like and what had brought them to London. Did any of them have families far away who'd also disowned them?

She'd been walking for some time when she realized the buildings on either side of the street were no longer familiar. Ada stopped and turned in a slow circle, the first niggling of alarm tightening her throat. Had she missed their street?

A boy of about nine or ten smacked into her, nearly making her drop her basket of food. "Are you hurt?" she asked as they both straightened.

He didn't respond. Instead, he gazed at her with large, vacant eyes, then darted a look over his shoulder. Without a word, he attempted to step around her.

"Do you live near here?" If he did, he might be able to help her find her way home.

The boy shrugged his bony shoulders.

"Would you, by chance, know the way to Burns Road?" she tried next.

His expression immediately changed from disinterested to cunning. "I might. But it'll cost a tanner."

Ada frowned. Could she trust him to give her the information once she handed over the sixpence? "Very well." Lifting her purse from the basket, she fished out the silver coin.

Instead of looking triumphant, the boy peered once more in the direction he'd come, and his face drained of color. "Keep yer tanner." He scurried forward and into a nearby alleyway.

Frustration and fear drove Ada to follow. She was hopelessly lost and needed someone's help to find her way home. "How about two tanners?" she called after him as she hurried down the alley. It was all the money she had after the trip to the market. "I need to find Burns . . ."

Her plea faded to stunned silence when she stepped from the alleyway into a crowded courtyard. A foul smell assaulted her senses, making Ada want to wretch. Everywhere she looked, she saw children with dirty faces and ragged clothing. Their mothers didn't appear to be faring much better. Several stared in her direction, their eyes as haunted as the boy's earlier. The air around her felt cold and oppressive. She shivered as she hugged her basket to her rapidly pounding heart.

"What do we 'ave 'ere?" A woman with disheveled brown hair approached her, a baby in a soiled gown resting on her hip. The deep lines of the mother's face made her age difficult for Ada to determine.

She swallowed hard. "I . . . uh . . ."

"'Ere to do your Christian duty, are ya? Or ya 'ere to gawk at us in pity?"

Shaking her head, Ada fell back a step. "I fear I'm quite lost."

"That'd be the truth," the woman remarked, her tone harsh. But some of the hardness dropped from her expression as she studied Ada further. "Where are ya needin' to go?"

Ada couldn't help glancing at the baby. Boy or girl, the babe's cheeks were far too gaunt. "Burns Road."

"You are turned around, aren't ya?" The woman sniffed with obvious amusement. Then to Ada's surprise, she explained the way to the flat.

"Thank you for your help." Ada took another step backward, anxious to leave this dismal place behind. "I truly appreciate it."

She started to turn, when her glance fell on the basket she still carried. "Wait," Ada said on impulse to the other woman as she wheeled back around.

The stranger raised her eyebrows in silent question.

"I have a bit of meat and vegetables." Ada reached into the basket and lifted out the food as proof. "It isn't much, but . . ."

The woman's eyes widened, yet she made no move to accept the offering. "I don't want no pity." The words were tinged with bitterness.

"I assure you, it isn't that." Ada stepped toward her. "I

have more than I need for supper. Please, accept it. For your little one there."

Gazing down at her baby, the mother pressed her thin lips into a tight line. Ada thought she saw the woman's chin begin to tremble. "I'll take it for 'im," she finally said. She maneuvered the baby so she could grasp the food Ada handed her.

"From one woman hoping to survive life in the city to another," Ada added in a quiet voice.

She'd been raised to believe those in poverty were beneath others, but in this moment, she felt a strong bond with this stranger. In many ways, they weren't so different from each other.

The woman's features softened briefly at Ada's words. "Thank you," she whispered. Then she spun around, calling curtly over her shoulder, "Ya'd best be goin' now, miss."

Ada retraced her way back through the alley. She blinked as she traded the dimness for the brighter light of the main street. The noise and bustle rushed to encircle her, propelling her forward, but none of it could penetrate her dazed state. Warring emotions vied for dominance inside her as she walked along—regret at not having more to give, relief at the thought of returning to her and Ned's small yet clean flat, and empathy for the uncertainty and distress in the woman's gaze.

Housekeeping and cooking no longer felt like weighty, impossible tasks to be performed each day. And her meat pies, burnt or not, now sounded as fine to Ada as a king's feast.

Ned bounded up the stairs to the flat. He was eager to tell Ada all about his first day at his new position.

There'd been moments of anxiety, to be sure, when he wasn't certain he'd ever learn how to operate the various pieces of equipment with ease. After all, he'd spent years learning gamekeeping under his father's tutelage before he'd taken over. By late afternoon, though, after his dinner of last night's leftovers, Ned felt more confident. Especially when the shop owner complimented him on how quickly he'd taken to the new tasks.

Turning the door handle, Ned found it didn't budge. Puzzled, he tried again. The door was locked, which meant Ada wasn't home. But where had she gone? A flicker of alarm shot through him at the thought of her wandering around the city, lost and alone. Perhaps she'd only retraced their walk from the day before.

Ned turned and headed back outside to wait for her. Others were returning from work as well. He nodded politely to several of the workmen and exchanged a few pleasantries with the chap who lived below him and Ada.

Still, Ned's concern expanded to dread when their conversation ended and Ada still hadn't appeared. Not knowing which way she'd gone, he headed down the line of tenement buildings until he reached the corner. Ada was nowhere in sight.

He returned the way he'd come and walked swiftly past their flat in the opposite direction. While there were still plenty of people about, the crowds were thinning as the supper hour began.

Then Ned saw her. Holding a basket at her side, Ada walked slowly, sorrow emanating from her expression and downcast eyes.

Did her grief have anything to do with the letter from her grandmother yesterday? Ada had shared little of its contents, other than to say her parents hadn't come round yet. Ned's jaw tightened anew at the thought. Though he didn't fault the Thornes for wanting their daughter to marry someone of equal station, he didn't agree with the way they'd handled their disappointment.

Ada lifted her chin. "Oh, you've come home," she said as Ned approached her.

He pressed a kiss to her cheek. "Where have you been, love?"

"I returned to the market to purchase a few more things." She hoisted her basket, but there was nothing inside. "Then I became lost..."

His apprehension returned. "You were lost?" He looked her up and down to reassure himself that she wasn't hurt. Other than a dirty hem, though, she looked hale and whole.

"A woman helped me..." Ada's voice shook with emotion, and she hurried to cover her mouth with her hand.

Not caring they were in public, Ned tugged her into his arms. "What's the matter, Ada?"

"I've never seen anything like it."

When she didn't expound, he gently suggested, "Why not start at the beginning?"

She nodded against his jacket.

As Ned guided her toward the flat, she shared how she'd burned her meat pies and had decided to go to the market for new ingredients. Ada told him about the boy she'd thought might be of help and how she'd followed him.

Ned trailed her up the stairs, but outside the door, Ada's energy seemed to give out. She sank onto the top step before he could put the key in the lock.

"It was the most awful place, Ned." Her horror and distress were unmistakable. "The smell and the refuse..." She shuddered as he sat beside her. "Far worse was the haunted look on their faces, even the children. Especially the children."

Placing his arm around her shoulders, Ned tucked her securely against his side. Guilt cut through him. He'd hoped to shelter Ada from ever witnessing such poverty, yet he hadn't succeeded, and it was only their second day in London.

"The woman accused me of coming to gawk at them," Ada continued, "or that I was only there to assuage my guilty Christian conscience." She tucked her head against his collar. "I told her that I had lost my way, and she was kind enough to share how to locate our road. But when I turned to leave . . ."

She began to weep, prompting him to hold her tighter. He'd never seen her cry before. "I realized we could eat burnt meat pies every night if we must. That's why I gave her my meat and vegetables." Ada brushed at her wet cheeks with her gloved hand. "I feared she wouldn't accept the food, but at long last she did, for the sake of her little one."

"Oh, Ada." Her compassion didn't surprise him—he'd witnessed it enough himself—but it pleased Ned to know she hadn't clung to the upper class's view of those in need.

She eased back to look at him, and the worry in her dark eyes pulled at his heart. "I'm sorry if it was terribly wasteful to purchase more food to replace what I ruined."

"I don't fault you, love," he said, hoping to allay the burden he could still see that she carried. "And I'll eat burnt pies. Tonight and any night, if needs be." He meant it, too. So long as they were together.

She gave him a tremulous smile, but it was a smile all the same. "I'm relieved to hear that."

"We can scrape off the worst of the scorching." Ned rose to his feet and helped her onto hers. "Then we'll thank the Lord for a decent meal and ask Him to bless that woman and her family."

Instead of deepening her smile as he'd hoped, Ada's lips drooped into a frown, her brow furrowed. "Does God truly care for them?"

"Of course."

"Why then would He allow them to live in such deplorable circumstances?"

Ned considered how to answer such a question. It wasn't so different than one he'd asked himself as a boy about the unfairness of families like the Whittingtons having far more than others. He could still recall most of his mother's words from that day.

"God doesn't measure worth or His care on His children being rich or poor." Ned brushed a strand of Ada's dark hair from her smooth cheek. "He knows our circumstances, whatever they be, can teach us lessons and help us grow."

His wife appeared to think over his response. "I want to understand such things, truly. But I'm afraid I don't, not fully. I still find it rather unfair and upsetting to know people not so very far away are living in that awful place."

"I can't say I don't agree."

Her brow crinkled further. "Then how can it be upsetting and unfair, yet not unmerciful of God?"

"Well . . ." Ned tugged on the brim of his cap. Could he explain it better? "When things are going well, we sometimes aren't as willing to turn to God or to try to be like Him."

Ada dipped her head in a slow nod. "I suppose that makes sense."

"No matter if we meet with ease or hardship, we all have a choice as to what to do with our lives." He unlocked the door and opened it. "We can let what happens lead us toward God or away from Him."

"I see." She threw him a pained look. "Though I'm not certain I'll ever fully understand faith the way you do."

He held her in a lingering hug. "Do you want to?"

"Yes," Ada answered after a moment.

"That's where faith starts—in the wanting."

Ned released her to see that her expression had turned less troubled, but all of her grief hadn't vanished. Her encounter in the slums had thrown a shadow over her, one that pained him to see.

"Shall we eat?" she asked with a cheeriness he could tell was forced. "I believe we can salvage at least two of my pies."

"Brilliant, because we're going to need every last bite."

One of her eyebrows arched. "Why is that?"

"Because," Ned said as he led her by the hand into the kitchen area, "after supper, we're going for a long walk until we learn every street and lane around the flat. That way, neither of us'll get lost."

She chuckled. "Then we may need to eat all six burnt pies."

Ned returned her cheeky smile, though it fell from his mouth the instant Ada moved toward the range. He might not have been able to prevent his wife's upsetting experience today or its consequences, but he would do all in his power to protect her from others in the future.

Chapter 4

ONCE ADA OVERCAME her initial bone-weary exhaustion at keeping house and cooking, she began to find satisfaction in it. Whenever she was tempted to sit down and cry over a ruined meal or her clumsy ironing, she reminded herself of what she'd seen in the slums her second day in the city and that Ned did not expect perfection from her.

She could—and would—do whatever work was required to keep a home for the two of them.

Their nightly walks, which had begun as a means to familiarize them both with their area of London, soon became a habit, a treasured time to talk about their days. In contrast to Ada's occasional struggles with her new tasks, Ned's work at the printer's was going well. That was something else Ada felt relieved about.

There was only one blight to her happiness—the continued silence from her parents. Every time she received a letter from her grandmother, Ada couldn't keep her hopes from soaring that this time, she would hear that her parents had changed their minds. And each time the news didn't come, more resentment chipped away at her hope and pushed her grief a little deeper inside her.

One overly warm day in July, two months after their arrival in London, Ada felt unwell after waking. Twice, before and after breakfast, she'd run to the bath scullery to ease the nausea in her stomach.

"Perhaps I should have skipped breakfast altogether," she murmured to herself as she rinsed the tub with water for the second time.

She hoped Ned wouldn't become ill. They needed every penny he earned.

Rising to her feet, she took a moment to steady herself against the doorframe. The queasiness had abated some, but she still longed to return to bed. Back home, she would have done just that, but here, she had far too much to do to be ill.

Ada gritted her teeth as she changed into one of her dresses. The lace on this particular gown refused to give up its yellowed appearance, no matter how diligently she scrubbed it. All of her clothes were similarly worn out by now. She'd even traded her fine corsets for plain, boneless ones the month before, to allow greater ease of movement in completing her daily tasks.

Once dressed, she sat at the vanity her grandmother had sent as a late wedding gift. Arranging her hair without help had presented her with another difficulty in the beginning, but soon, Ada had learned to manage it alone.

Her rosy cheeks were long gone, replaced by a pale thinness that made her dark eyes appear twice as large. Ned claimed she was as beautiful as ever, even when she was up to her elbows in soap suds or had flour dotting her nose. And she loved him all the more for it.

With her hair up and off her neck, Ada stripped the sheets and blankets from the bed in preparation for washing day. A knock at the door startled her. They never had visitors, except for their landlord—and it wasn't yet time for the rent to be collected. The absence of others to talk with during the day had been difficult for Ada, but she'd grown accustomed to it, and it made her and Ned's walks all the more precious.

The person knocked again. Ada moved from the bedroom, through the main room, and down the short hallway. She opened the door to find a woman standing on the stairs, a baby propped on her hip. The stranger had fiery red hair and appeared to be a few years older than Ada.

"Morning. Name's Minnie O'Reilly." A slight Irish accent wound its way beneath the woman's London brogue. "Me and mine moved into the building next door just last week." Smiling, she shifted the baby to the other hip, revealing a young girl clinging to her skirts. "I 'eard another woman lived in this flat, so I thought we'd come over and—"

Without warning, Ada's stomach churned with a new wave of sickness. "I'm so sorry . . ." Her cheeks flushed with mortification as she darted through the scullery door behind her and hurried to close it. She barely made it to the bathtub to vomit a third time.

She tried to stand when she was done, but her feet and legs felt too shaky to move. Ada leaned her head against the side of the tub, her embarrassment giving way to annoyance. Hot tears blurred her vision, increasing her frustration. She'd been a weepy mess the last few weeks.

"Ma'am?" A soft tap sounded on the scullery door. "You unwell?"

Using the side of the tub for help, Ada climbed to her feet. "A bit, but I'm hoping it will pass soon. You're more than welcome to call again later in the week . . ."

"'Ow long have you been feelin' this way?" Minnie asked, poking her head inside the small room.

Ada blinked in surprise at the rather personal question. "The past week or two." When Minnie stepped back into the hallway, Ada followed.

"Is it just smells what makes you ill, or food, too?"

"Both."

"My guess is you've also been cryin' more than normal."

Ada's eyes widened at the woman's perceptiveness. "Yes." Clearly, Minnie knew a great deal about various sicknesses. "Whatever is the matter with me?" She clasped her hands together, hoping it wasn't too serious. "My husband has not been ill at all."

Minnie's laugh rang bright and friendly. "It's not likely 'e'll catch what you 'ave, ma'am."

"Please. Call me Ada." She pressed one hand against her high collar, steeling herself for the prognosis. "And what, pray tell, do you believe I have that he doesn't?"

Minnie gave her a kind smile. "I'm guessin' you're with child, Ada."

"With . . . child?" An astonished chuckle escaped her lips. Now that she thought about it, she had missed her monthly bleeding, but she'd been too busy to notice. "I am going to have a baby?" She shook her head in wonder.

"Here. Hold William." Minnie held the baby out to Ada, who reluctantly took him into her arms. Her experience with babies was relatively nonexistent. "Me and Janey will go fix you up a cup of tea, what'll 'ave you feeling better in no time." With that, Minnie shuffled her clingy daughter out the door.

Ada gazed at the baby. He was sucking on the ends of his loose bonnet strings. Smoothing his nightdress, she bounced him a bit. Immediately, William dropped the ribbons and gurgled, revealing a single tooth.

"Do you find that amusing, little one?" She bounced him again and was rewarded with a giggle. The happy noise went straight to her heart. Wouldn't Ned be so pleased to hear she was going to have a baby? Their flat would soon be home to three.

She carried William into the parlor, where she pointed out the knickknacks, books, and furniture she and Ned had purchased. The baby babbled back as though carrying on a conversation. By the time Ada had finished giving him a tour of the flat, his mother and sister had returned with a steaming cup of tea. The smell alone soothed Ada's stomach.

After handing back the baby to Minnie, Ada led the way to the kitchen table. They each took a seat on one of the chairs. After a minute, Minnie convinced Janey to sit as well.

"Thank you for the tea and for helping me realize why I've been unwell." Ada blushed at her own naiveté, though she couldn't stop smiling, either.

She was going to have a baby—perhaps a light-brown-haired boy like Ned, or a dark-eyed girl like herself. Son or daughter, she would teach this dear child all that she'd learned and observed in the past few months about love, compassion, and the fulfillment found in hard work. Another thought deepened Ada's smile. Surely, her parents would write to her once they knew they had a grandchild.

Ada sipped some of the tea and breathed a contented sigh. "Your visit was more than fortuitous, Minnie."

It was Minnie's turn to blush. "Don't know what a fancy word like that means. But I'm 'appy to 'elp." She reached out and patted Ada's hand where it held the cup. "Anything you need, Ada, you let me know. Cause I 'ave a feeling you and me, we're going to be great friends."

As Ned greeted his wife tonight with his usual kiss to her cheek, he was struck by the radiance of her smile.

"How was your day?" she asked as she moved about the kitchen, putting the finishing touches on their supper.

He moved to the sink to wash his hands, knowing full well that some of the ink smudges would remain no matter how much he lathered his fingertips. Back in Yorkshire, his hands had been covered with a different sort of stain from tending the game animals on the estate, clearing away brush, or tramping through the wet woods in search of poacher traps.

There were days when he longed to be outdoors as he used to be. Rain or shine, he'd spent every day outside before coming to London. Ned lifted his gaze to peer at their tiny garden. He missed the fresh, damp scent of the earth and the stillness that came with walking in the woods alone.

Hearing Ada behind him, he smiled and scrubbed harder at his hands. He wouldn't trade the potent smell of the print shop or the whir of its machines for his old job. Not if it meant losing his lovely Ada.

"Ned? Did you hear me?"

He hadn't answered her question yet about his day. "Sorry. Things at the shop are busy. We finished a large order and have two more to fill." He grabbed a nearby towel to dry his hands and turned to face her. "How was your day, love?"

"It went well. Very well, actually."

When she didn't elaborate, he eyed her curiously. "What? No other bits to share? Are you waiting for our walk?"

"Not exactly," Ada replied in an innocent tone, but he saw the way her dark eyes shone with amusement.

Ned waited until she'd finished setting the table before he snagged hold of her wrist. "All right now. What aren't you saying?"

"I am sure I don't know what you mean, Mr. Henley." She threw him a cheeky grin.

Feigning a growl of protest, he tickled her in the side. Ada squealed with laughter. "Ready to up and confess now, Mrs. Henley?"

"Never," she said in between laughs.

Grinning, he tickled her some more.

"Oh, very well. I surrender."

He curled his arm around her waist. "You'd make a poor soldier, I'm afraid," he teased as he kissed the skin below her ear.

"Quite true." She looped her arms around his neck. "Besides, I would never wish to leave you . . . and our baby . . . to join the ranks."

He bent to kiss her mouth, but he straightened in surprise when her words registered in his mind. "Wait. Did you say *our baby?*"

"Indeed." Ada rewarded him with another beaming smile. "I believe I'm pregnant. Minnie O'Reilly, our new neighbor, believes the same. It was she who helped me realize why I've felt unwell and weepy lately. Ned, we're going to have a baby."

He was going to be a father. They were going to be parents!

"Are you pleased?" Ada asked, slight worry in her tone.

Ned lifted his hands to cup her beautiful face. "More than pleased. I'm overjoyed. You'll be such a fine mum."

"And you a fine daddy."

He kissed her fervently. When they parted, they were both breathless. Ned led her to the table. Tonight, he kept her hand in his as he gave thanks for their meal. Before ending the prayer, he added, "Father, bless Ada and the little one we believe she's carrying . . ." Ada squeezed his hand, prompting tears of gratitude and anticipation to fill Ned's eyes. He had to clear his throat before continuing. "We're indeed grateful for all we have, and close in Thy Son's name. Amen."

To his surprise, Ada softly echoed his "*amen.*" It was the first time he could recall her doing so—and the sweetness of it added to his overflowing joy.

Ada's daily sickness, which had largely been held in check by Minnie's tea, eventually disappeared as quickly as it had come—to her great joy. She felt less tired, too, in performing her household tasks. Or perhaps her energy had more to do with her inner contentment. Though there were days when she wondered how she could wring one more penny from Ned's wages, or when she and Minnie had to pool or trade their foodstuff with each other, Ada couldn't help feeling happy. She would have a baby next year, a little bundle of energy and personality like Little William. And she couldn't wait.

"Can you believe we have lived here four months already?" she remarked to Ned during one of their evening strolls about London.

He shook his head. "Seems half as short and twice as long."

"My sentiments exactly." She laughed and linked her arm more securely through his, feeling proud to be walking beside him. "Have you given any more thought to what we ought to name the baby?"

Her husband squinted up at the gray sky. The cooler air felt wonderful to Ada after the heat of working over the range to prepare supper.

"I like Ned Jr. if we have a boy."

Ada nodded in agreement. "And if we have a girl?"

"Maud or Lucille are nice." He sneaked a kiss to her cheek. "Though I still prefer Ada."

His remark drew a smile from her. "Any others you've thought of?"

"One."

She waited for him to continue. When he didn't, and she realized he was purposely drawing out the suspense, Ada gently elbowed him in the side. "If you'd be so kind as to share it aloud, Ned, dear."

"It's the name my mum said she would've given her daughter if she'd had one."

"What is it?" Ada asked, intrigued.

Ned stopped her at the corner to let a bus pass by, its upper level boasting an advertisement for Pears soap. "It's Rosemary. That was the middle name of one of my grans, and Mum always liked it."

"Rosemary," Ada repeated. "You know, I believe that one is my favorite."

"Truly?" They crossed the street. "The others are fine names, too."

"Yes, but Rosemary is quite beautiful." She gazed up at him, a fresh wave of love filling her. "Our own little rose—if the baby's a girl."

He grinned. "That's what we'll call her for short."

"Rose?"

"No, too stiff. I was thinking Rosie."

"Oh, that's perfect, Ned." She squeezed his arm.

Their conversation turned to the things they'd need to procure before the baby's arrival, such as a cradle. Ada watched a mother on the opposite side of the street pushing a perambulator. Perhaps they could find a pram that wouldn't cost too much. Minnie had volunteered to stitch some nightgowns and a blanket, while her husband, Thomas, who was an expert at whittling, had promised to make a small toy that the child could eventually play with.

"It's our turn to have the O'Reillys to dine . . ." A sudden pain in her back had Ada pulling in a sharp breath.

Ned glanced down at her as he slowed to a stop. "Something wrong, love?"

"Only a bit of soreness. I imagine it's from doing the wash earlier."

Still, it had been some time since she'd experienced the aches and pains that had first accompanied her daily tasks. This discomfort felt different, too. A pestering fear, one Ada tried to block out with reminders that she'd likely only bent down too much today, wouldn't cease harassing her thoughts. But she didn't want to worry Ned, especially if her concerns were entirely unfounded.

"Shall we head back?" he asked, his expression worried nonetheless.

She attempted a reassuring smile, even as the aching in her back returned. "It might be nice to lie down."

They turned in tandem and headed back the way they'd come. Ada was grateful Ned carried the conversation, seeming to notice that she no longer felt much like talking. She did her best to listen and comment, but as the pain in her back increased in strength, so did her fear.

Chapter 5

"Is there nothing more you can do for her?" Through the partly opened door, Ned could see Ada hadn't moved since the doctor had completed his examination. She lay on their bed, facing the opposite wall, her pale face contrasting sharply with her dark hair. His heart twisted painfully in his chest at the sight.

The doctor put on his hat and shook his head. "She's young, but she's strong and will likely have another baby in time."

"Why did she lose . . . this baby?" The last word scraped against Ned's throat. He could hardly believe he'd left for the print shop this morning still thinking he'd be a father in a matter of months, and then discovered Ada bleeding and in pain when he'd returned home. He knew all about birth and life and death. But unlike some forest creature he had a mild fondness for, this was his wife.

Could her hard work around the house, something she'd never had to do before marrying him, be the cause of her miscarriage? Would she have kept the baby if they'd been living back in Yorkshire? The possibility tore at him. Ned ran his hand through his already disheveled hair.

"Unfortunately, these things simply happen."

Ned followed the doctor through the main room toward the door. Minnie glanced at them from where she worked at the range, finishing the preparations for supper that Ada had started earlier.

"What of the London air?" he asked quietly. "Should my wife stay indoors next time? Or do less work?" They couldn't afford a servant, but they'd manage somehow if it meant Ada was able to carry another baby.

"Mr. Henley," the doctor said in a gentle tone, "miscarriages occur everywhere on God's earth—in the most populated of cities and in the fresh air of the countryside. And one encounter, however difficult, is not an indication that you ought to move or even that your wife will miscarry again."

The man's pragmatic statement eased some of the guilt Ned had been harboring all evening. "Thank you, sir." He paid the doctor, shook his hand, and saw him on his way.

"'Ow is she?" Minnie asked in a low voice when Ned returned to the kitchen.

Pocketing his hands, he lifted his shoulders in a helpless shrug. "The doctor believes she'll recover soon enough. But . . ." He coughed as his lungs tightened with fresh pain. "I've not ever seen her this low, Minnie. Not even when she knew she'd lose her parents once she married me."

"I 'eard what the doctor said just now. Ada's strong." She squeezed his shoulder in a comforting gesture. "You both are. You'll get through by and by. In the meantime, supper's ready."

He thanked her as he followed her to the door of the flat. Trepidation and helplessness soured his stomach when he shut the door behind her. Both the doctor and Minnie seemed so confident in their knowledge and assistance. But what about him? How could he help his beloved Ada?

Slowly, he moved to the bedroom and pushed the door fully open. Ada's gaze didn't stir from the wall. "Minnie made supper. Would you care for some, love?"

"No, thank you." Her whisper barely reached his ears.

Truth be told, he wasn't feeling all that peckish, either. The haunted look in Ada's tearless eyes compelled him to her side. To avoid jostling her aching body, he grabbed a chair from the kitchen and positioned it beside the bed.

"I'm ever so sorry, Ada." He reached out to clasp her fingers. They felt cold. "I know how much you—how much we—wanted this child."

She shut her eyes against what he suspected was another wave of grief.

"The doctor says you're strong," he tried next. "And that living here isn't what brought on the loss."

Breaking his hold, she rolled onto her other side, her back now to him. He longed to scoop her into his arms and hold her as she cried. But he hesitated, afraid of hurting her or upsetting her further.

"Can I bring you anything? A book? Some water?"

She shook her head, but the movement was nearly imperceptible, and Ned would've missed it if he hadn't been watching her.

"I could read to you."

Again, he caught the slight shake of her head.

It was agony to see her so lost in her heartache, however appropriate. "I suppose I'll try some supper after all."

There was no answer, no movement, other than the steady rise and fall of her rounded shoulders as she breathed in and out. Ned lifted the chair and carried it to the door, where he paused.

"Ada?" He didn't turn, afraid he'd read condemnation in the lines of her back. "Do you blame me?"

A long moment passed with nothing but the muted sounds of the city on the other side of the window to fill in the stillness. Then he heard her faint reply. "No."

He should've felt relief at her answer as he served himself some food and sat alone at the table. But he couldn't shake off the shadows inside his own mind, telling him that he *was* to blame. After all, what did he expect after bringing a delicate young woman like Ada to the city? She'd endured the hard work admirably. But at what cost—that of their baby and Ada's health and happiness?

They'd come to London to create a home of their own, but if that dream could not be realized . . . Hanging his head, Ned silently poured out his anguish to the Lord as his tears struck the untouched meal on his plate.

Ada stood up from the table and took her half-empty cup of tea to the sink for washing. A week had passed since . . . She shut her eyes against the pain that immediately lanced her heart. Would it ever go away? There were moments when she felt trapped in a state of numbness, while other times, she hurt so much inside she could hardly breathe. The beautiful little baby she and Ned had talked and dreamt about would not be coming after all.

"Sure you're not wantin' another biscuit now?" Minnie asked from where she sat at the table.

Janey was entertaining William in the parlor. The sound of his happy laughter was as much a balm to Ada's flagging spirits as it was a painful reminder of what she'd lost.

"No, thank you."

Minnie's shortbread was the most delicious Ada had ever

tasted, but one biscuit had been enough. Especially when she and Ned had mostly been subsiding on toast. Minnie had graciously helped clean the flat the day before, giving Ada one more day in bed, but Ned wasn't overly skilled in the kitchen in Ada's absence.

She ran the water over the teacup, watching the dark liquid wash away. Just like her baby's life had. The thought had her gripping the edge of the sink with one hand. She'd expected tears like the ones she'd seen in Ned's eyes that first night before he'd gone to sleep on the sofa to allow her more room. Yet her eyes remained dry.

"I know 'ow you're feelin', Ada."

Setting down the cup, she turned and looked at Minnie in surprise. "You had a miscarriage?"

"After Janey and 'fore William." Her friend's gaze grew wistful. "It gets better—to where it don't 'urt so much. But you still wonder. What would they 'ave been like?"

Ada stared down at her dress. No one had likely suspected she'd been pregnant. Her stomach had barely begun to expand.

"It's the talkin' what 'elps," Minnie added. "You can talk to me. Or to Ned."

A lump clogged her throat when Ada thought of her husband. He was still sleeping on the sofa in the parlor. When they spoke in the evenings now, their conversations were short, composed of simple questions about her health and his day at the printer's. Neither of them mentioned the baby.

"I'm afraid Ned blames himself," she admitted. "For bringing me here."

Minnie gave a thoughtful nod. "Do you blame 'im?"

"No, of course not. I told him as much. But . . ."

Her friend lifted her eyebrows. "But?"

"Oh, Minnie, I fear he blames *me*." She sank back down

into her chair. "I wished to come to London more than Ned did. He understood how much better things would be for our children if we raised them away from Stonefield Hall. But what if we're unable to have a family? Will he wish he'd never left Yorkshire? Or married me?" She glanced around at the flat, its walls pressing in on her as they hadn't since her first month here.

Reaching out, Minnie squeezed her hand. "Do you regret marryin' 'im?"

"Not for a single moment." And Ada meant it. Even during those hours when she'd been so far gone in her grief she didn't think she would ever find her way back out, she felt no regret at marrying Ned.

Minnie picked up her teacup again and took a sip. "'Ave you told 'im that of late?"

The question caught Ada by surprise before it pierced straight through her anguish. "No," she said, shaking her head. "Though I imagine he knows how I feel about him."

"'E may or 'e may not." Her friend set the teacup in its saucer. Recently, Ada had saved enough to purchase a matching set of four. "I've come to learn a man takes it 'ard when 'is woman is distressed. They're wantin' to protect us, and they 'ate it when they can't."

Was that how Ned felt? Ada's own mourning had felt too thick and heavy to clearly see anyone else's. Remorse coursed through her at the realization she hadn't thought to ask how her husband might be suffering.

A longing to speak to him, in the way they used to and not in the stilted conversations of the past week, filled her to distraction. There were still two hours to go before he came home, though, and that was if he arrived on time. He'd stayed a bit later than usual the past two nights to finish a large order.

"I'll tell him tonight," she resolved aloud. And something

akin to anticipation flickered faintly inside her for the first time all week.

Having been on her feet longer than she had in seven days, Ada fell asleep while waiting for Ned. She woke to darkness. A peek inside the parlor showed her that Ned had returned and was sleeping himself. She would have to wait to talk with him tomorrow morning.

However, when Ada woke the next day, Ned was already gone. Disappointed, she dressed and made herself breakfast. Since Minnie had already completed the cleaning, Ada decided to tackle the mending basket. It was one skill she'd taken up with ease, having been tutored by her mother at a young age on how to effectively wield a needle and thread. Though these days, her stitching projects consisted of patching holes in Ned's trousers and darning socks.

She worked in the parlor beside the open window. It felt good to hear the city alive and thriving beyond the flat. At the bottom of the basket, she found the bonnet she'd started sewing for the baby. Ned must have stowed it there, out of sight.

Running her fingers over the white material, Ada felt a resurgence of her loss and longing. What would her mother say about the miscarriage? Victoria Thorne had only had one child. Was that because she, too, had experienced the loss of a baby? Ada suddenly wished she knew—that the silence between them wasn't such a barrier. Tears lodged in her throat, yet they wouldn't come.

Should she throw out the tiny bonnet? She held it tight, considering. Then, like Ned, she tucked it back beneath the pile of mending.

Why had her husband put the bonnet there? Was it to keep the painful reminder away from her . . . or from himself? The desire to ask him felt as persistent and pressing as her pain had been earlier in the week.

The hours slowly ticked by. Ada managed to prepare a simple supper. She hoped Ned would be pleased to eat something other than tea and toast again. At last, the time came for his arrival home. Ada waited in the parlor with a book to ensure she didn't miss him this time, whether she fell asleep or not.

However, the hour grew later, the light outside dimmer, his supper colder, and still, Ned didn't come. Alarm she hadn't felt so keenly since that day they'd met at the train station in Scotland returned in full force. Was her husband still at the shop? Or had something happened to him? Ada tried reading, but the words could only hold her attention for a few minutes before she glanced at the mantel clock again.

With slightly trembling fingers, she changed into her nightgown. Perhaps Ned had wanted to finish the print job tonight, regardless of how late it became. Ada didn't like the idea of him walking home after dark, though.

The sound of the outer door creaking open sent her heart thrashing in relief. She stepped quickly from the bedroom to see Ned walking into the kitchen, his head down, his shoulders stooped.

"You're home!"

Ned jerked his chin up, his eyes widening when he saw her. "Ada? I thought you'd be in bed."

"I wanted to wait for you." She offered him what she hoped resembled a smile.

He shot her a wary look. "Something wrong?"

"No." She shook her head. "I only hoped to . . ." As he removed his coat, she caught the scent of ale wafting off him.

Ada froze, her stomach twisting with sick realization. "You were not at the shop, were you?"

He glanced away. "I was for a bit."

"You went to a pub." She crossed her arms.

She hadn't phrased her words as a question, but Ned nodded anyway, his gaze still avoiding hers.

"Are you drunk, Ned?" Ada hardly dared believe it, but the proof seemed to be before her. Was this a habit he'd taken up recently, or one he'd hidden from her since the beginning?

He finally looked at her. Yet instead of remorse, his blue eyes flashed with anger. "I had a single pint."

She was relieved to hear it, though she still felt confused. "Why didn't you come home right away? I made us supper." She waved a hand at the plate on the table. "Are you angry at having to eat only toast most days?"

"It's got nothing to do with toast." Ned removed his cap and stood staring at it.

The silence between them hung tense and suffocating. "Why did you go to the pub instead of returning straight home?"

"I needed time."

Ada sensed what he didn't say—he'd needed time away from her. She pressed her folded arms against the yawning hurt his statement inspired. "I see. And is there a reason you couldn't simply tell me as much? Why is it you refuse to talk to me?"

"Refuse to talk to you?" His tone, while pained, held an incredulous edge to it, too. "I've tried for days to talk to you, Ada. You're the one who refuses. You've been so consumed by what happened that you won't talk."

"I lost a baby," she countered, her ire covering her pain.

Ned's expression softened slightly, but his reply still had the power to wound. "I lost a baby . . . and a wife."

She opened her mouth to argue, to inflict the same cutting pain she felt. How had their relationship come to this—accusations and cloistered hurts? A sudden thought had Ada pressing her lips together. Throwing a barb at Ned wouldn't fix things between them. If anything, it would surely make them worse now that she realized he was hurting every bit as much as her. Was it little wonder he'd spent his hours somewhere else tonight?

Minnie's words from yesterday returned to her mind—*they're wantin' to protect us, and they 'ate it when they can't.* A wave of regret washed through her, purging her anger.

"You are correct." She took a deep breath and hazarded a step toward him. "I have been consumed with my own pain. And for that, I'm truly sorry, Ned. I was just so happy, so certain we would have this . . ."

She couldn't finish the sentence. The tears she'd believed would never come filled her eyes and spilled over onto her cheeks. In the next moment, Ned was cradling her against him. Ada couldn't recall anything feeling as wonderful, or as safe, as his arms around her.

"I believed so, too, love," he murmured, his hand running the length of her unfettered hair.

Her crying was as bitter as it was cleansing. "Am I being punished for some failure? Why did God take our baby?"

"I . . ." Ned cleared his throat. "I don't have all the answers, love." His kiss to her forehead was achingly tender. "I do know this—God isn't a punishing being, Ada. He weeps for us and with us. His love isn't just evident in the happy times. He's there with us in the sad ones, too. And He, alone, knows what a person needs to grow, even if that growth brings pain."

She pressed the side of her face against his shirtfront as she joined her hands behind his back. How she'd missed him!

And from the almost desperate way Ned held her in return, she knew he had missed her, too.

"I'm sorry for not coming home straightaway." He rested his chin on top of her head. "I didn't know if you wanted me around."

Ada tightened her grasp. "I always want you around."

"Truly?" He tilted her chin upward until their eyes met. "You don't ever wish you'd stayed in Yorkshire and married an earl?"

She was tempted to tease, but she sensed there was more seriousness than jest behind the question. "No, I do not wish I had married an earl. I longed to marry a man of integrity and kindness who would exemplify such values to our children." Another few tears slid down her face. Ned caught one with his thumb. "And that, Mr. Henley, is precisely what I did."

"You did warn me you were stubborn." There was a spark in his eyes that she hadn't seen in some time.

One corner of her mouth rose. "I did, didn't I? And I am stubborn enough to choose this life over and over again—whether it is just you and I or not."

The intense relief on his handsome face told her volumes of his own suffering over the last week. "From now on," Ned said, "we'll work through what comes, you and me, together. Promise?"

"I promise."

When their lips met, it was with a kiss as sweet and affectionate as their first had been beside the oak tree all those months ago. Yet unlike that kiss, this one also held deep grief over what they'd lost and a fragile hope for the future.

Chapter 6

November 1910

ADA FOUND THE letter at the bottom of the mending basket, beneath the half-finished baby bonnet she had come into the parlor to find. Withdrawing both, she sucked in a sharp breath at the address on the envelope. It took a moment to realize it wasn't from her mother—it was *to* her mother. Ada had written the missive a few weeks after her miscarriage, on an especially gray day when she'd longed to speak to her mother about the loss.

How Ned had managed to intercept the returned letter and hide it before she could find it, Ada was unsure. She did know what it meant that the missive had come back to her unopened. Her parents were still determined to have no contact with her.

Setting the letter aside, along with the wave of pain and anger that threatened to pull her under, she fingered the half-finished bonnet. A tiny smile tugged at her mouth. She would need to finish the little cap by next summer, if all went well. And she was hoping—maybe even praying—that things would go well this time.

The sound of the door opening had her hurrying to her feet. Ned was home! Ada met him in the kitchen with a kiss, but rather than setting the table as she usually did at that point, she led him toward the parlor.

"We aren't eating?" he said with a chuckle.

"In a moment."

He lifted his eyebrows in question, but she waited until he was seated in the armchair, his favorite seat, and she'd perched on his lap before explaining.

"I have news." Her heart beat as much with excitement as it did trepidation. Would Ned be happy at her announcement? "We are going to need this after all." She pressed the half bonnet into his hand.

Ned glanced from the cloth to her face, his eyes widening. "You're..."

"Yes." Ada nodded. "The doctor confirmed it today."

He pulled her against him. "That's brilliant, Ada." His lips brushed her forehead. "Right?"

"Very much so." She linked her fingers with his and gave them a squeeze. "Are you pleased? The doctor assured me it was not too soon."

Shifting, he peered at her directly. "I'm more than pleased. I'm overjoyed, love."

"As am I. But I'm also afraid." She fingered his collar with her free hand. "I don't wish to be, but I am. I so want to keep this baby and be a mother."

Ned encircled his arms around her waist. "I'm a bit scared, too, if I'm honest."

Hearing his admission eased some of Ada's anxiety.

"One more thing." She stood and collected the letter from where she'd set it on the sofa. "I found this." She held it up for him to see.

His expression changed at once, from elated to chagrined.

"Why would you hide it, Ned?" She was more perplexed than angry. After all, over the past two months, their relationship had been warmer and more open than ever before.

He lowered his gaze and rubbed his hand over the chair arm. "I didn't wish to upset you. You seemed to be doing better when the letter was sent back." When he lifted his head, his blue eyes were full of remorse and a plea for understanding. "I feared that seeing it would send you back... into that dark fog."

Ada didn't need to ask what he meant. A shiver ran through her at the memory of the deep grief that had held her prisoner for a time after her miscarriage. She hoped to never return to it again.

"Perhaps I would have returned to that bleak place."

Standing, he wrapped her in his arms. "Forgive me. I only wished to protect you."

"I know," she murmured, resting her head against his chest. "But you can't—not always. Besides, we promised one another that we would work together, remember?" She gazed up at him.

He hesitated a moment, then dipped his head in a nod. "We did."

"So come what may"—she kissed him—"we face it together. Which means no more sheltering me from every bit of trouble. Agreed?"

Ned pressed a kiss to her brow. "Agreed."

July 1911

Ned was certain he'd never seen any being as perfect in

form as his infant daughter. Rubbing a finger over her smooth cheek, he stared down in awe at her through watery eyes.

"She's lovely, Ada," he said hoarsely.

His wife's glowing smile, as tired as she was from the difficult task of bringing their baby into the world, rivaled any other Ned had seen on her sweet lips. "Rosemary Henley," Ada crooned to the baby she held in her arms. "Our little Rosie is a beauty, is she not?"

"As are you, love." From his seat next to her at the head of the bed, Ned bent forward and kissed her temple.

Her dark eyes were lit with love and joy as she glanced at him. "Thank you, Ned."

"For?" He'd accomplished little today, beyond wearing a rut into the floor with his pacing while the doctor and Minnie had attended to Ada. Then he'd heard the cry of the baby—*their baby*—and his nervousness had changed to instant elation and relief.

Ada leaned her head against him. "For marrying me."

He could think of no greater compliment than to hear that her own happiness matched his. The last year had not been as free of challenge as he would have liked for his Ada. But they were learning to pull together rather than apart. Ned hadn't hidden any more returned letters, though there'd been several over the past eight months.

Relying more on God was something else he'd been learning. Many nights during Ada's pregnancy, Ned had lain awake, worrying about her and the baby and hoping the result would be different from the last time. It had been in those moments when his silent prayers had flowed more deeply from his heart than ever before. While he couldn't protect Ada or their child from everything—he understood that now—he could try to surrender them and his fears to God.

"Would you care to hold her?" Ada asked.

Nodding, he carefully took the baby into his arms. He'd seen his fair share of newborn creatures during his time as a gamekeeper. But cradling his daughter to his chest was by far the most moving experience with new life that he'd witnessed.

Little Rosemary yawned in her sleep, prompting a smile from him. "She has your dark hair."

"Yes, but those are your blue eyes."

Ned touched the baby's nose. "They might not stay blue."

"Oh, they will," she said with confidence and an impish smile. "I am sure of it."

He chuckled. "I can't believe she's truly here."

"Nor I." As if she needed proof, Ada reached out and brushed Rosemary's hair. "Ned?" she said after a moment.

"Hmm?"

"Shall we... may we... say a prayer, of thanks?"

His gaze went to hers, though he did his best to check his surprise. "I'd like that." He cleared past the lump in his throat to begin, but Ada stopped him with a hand to his sleeve.

"May I say it?"

He did a poor job of hiding his astonishment this time, because Ada took one look at his expression and laughed lightly.

"I wish to say it, but only if that is fine with you."

He answered with a nod, not sure if he could have spoken even if he'd wished to. Bowing his head, he listened intently to her quiet words.

"Our Father in Heaven, we thank You for our little Rosemary." Her voice broke with emotion. Ned recognized it as the same joyful gratitude spilling through him. "She is beautiful and in good health, and we are indeed grateful to have her here with us. Bless her and guide us as her parents." Ada paused. When she continued, it was in a less certain tone, but one that was every bit as earnest. "If possible, Father, allow her birth to soften the hearts of my mother and father."

Ned placed his cheek against Ada's hair. He didn't blame her one bit for the hurt and anger she still felt toward Charles and Victoria Thorne. Yet, she also hoped to mend those relationships. He added his own hope for that reunion as he echoed Ada's "*amen.*"

"How was I? Did it sound right?" She looked up at him, her face full of expectation and concern.

He smiled reassuringly. "It was perfect."

And he wasn't just talking of her first prayer aloud. In the wake of Ada's tentative faith, the smell of Minnie's prepared supper scenting the air, his daughter held snugly in his arms, and his dear wife at his side, Ned knew what a perfect moment could be.

On an especially gray day in January, Ada stood at the parlor window, watching the rain pelt against the glass. It was only four in the afternoon, according to the clock, but it would be fully dark before Ned returned from the printing shop. Six months had come and gone since Rosemary's birth, though in many ways, Ada felt as if they'd always been a family of three.

She shivered in the room's cooler air, feeling more than ready for winter to end. Turning from the soggy view, she went into the bedroom to check on her daughter. Rosemary napped in the cradle, beneath the new blanket Minnie had recently sewn for her. The baby's pink lips moved in a suckling motion as she slept, coaxing a brief smile from Ada.

With supper baking inside the range and Rosemary sleeping, Ada had a rare moment to herself. But how to spend it? At home, there would have been teas or parties or even a chilly horse ride across the estate—with a suitable companion, of course—to occupy her time.

A lump of homesickness clogged her throat as she thought of Stonefield Hall. Nearly two years had passed since she'd left—and not a single reply from her parents. Ada had written them again at Christmastime, but their cold silence stretched on. She remained grateful for her regular correspondence with her grandmother, but it didn't fully fill the void left by her parents.

Why will not they write back instead of returning my letters? she asked herself yet again as she retraced her steps to the parlor. *Why can't they be happy for me, for us?*

Anger, raw and biting, rose inside her, pushing back at the chill she felt. She'd tried to understand her parents' disappointment. Yet how would they know that Ned was a good husband to her or that Ada had a daughter if they never opened her letters? Their accusations about Ada abandoning them and their way of life felt sharply ironic to her now. Who was really abandoning whom?

She marched to the nearby bookshelf, tugged a volume from it, and sat in Ned's armchair to read. The swirl of emotion within her—frustration, grief, and longing—couldn't be so easily ignored. She shut the book after a few moments, unable to concentrate.

Since having a child herself, Ada had missed her own mother even more. Of course, her experience with raising a child had and would continue to be vastly different from Victoria Thorne's. Ada had no nursemaid, nanny, or governess to help. And while she cherished Minnie's friendship and sage counsel, there were still questions she longed to ask her mother, questions Ada had penned within her letters—only to have them returned, sealed and unanswered.

Would her parents ever change their minds about her?

The painful uncertainty elicited a physical ache inside her. She loved Ned and Rosemary with all her heart. But this winter, caring for a growing baby along with her other responsibilities during the long, bleak days of cold weather had left her feeling far more despondent than she'd ever felt before in her life.

"What do I do?" she murmured aloud, disrupting the room's stillness. It was almost like a prayer, something she hadn't attempted since the day of Rosemary's birth.

While her parents' continual rejection hurt deeply, Ada still longed to be free of any lingering resentment and anger. Perhaps it was time to stop writing them. Would she be able to move through her grief if she was no longer confronted with their silent dismissal again and again?

A flicker of peace accompanied her thoughts and had Ada squaring her shoulders with new resolve. She wouldn't send any more letters for now. Instead, she would concentrate completely on her own marriage and family—and maybe even on the miniature seed of faith she'd sensed growing in her heart, too.

Still, was there something she might do to help these winter days pass more quickly? Her gaze shifted from the window to the trunk they still used as a makeshift table in the parlor. Her resources and funds might be limited, yet that didn't mean she couldn't think of new ways to add more color and laughter and conversation to her life.

An idea began to form, and it brought a smile to her mouth for more than just a moment or two. Moving to the trunk, Ada lifted the lid and pulled out the lace shawl she kept there. It would make the perfect tablecloth.

She spread the cloth over the trunk, then went to the kitchen to put on the kettle. It was the usual time of day for tea, but this afternoon would be different. From the cupboard, she withdrew three teacups and saucers instead of one and set them on a tray. She placed a few biscuits she had on hand onto a plate. Next, Ada pulled out her stationery and penned an official-looking invitation. She could hear the sounds of Rosemary stirring as she finished.

After feeding the baby, she bundled up Rosemary and carried her outside. The cold damp engulfed them as Ada knocked at Minnie's door. Janey answered with a smile. "Hello, Mrs. Henley," she said, stepping back to allow Ada to enter.

"Hello, Janey." Ada slipped inside, and the girl shut the door behind her. She presented the invitation to Minnie's daughter. "You and your mother and William are cordially invited to my ladies' teatime."

Minnie approached, wiping her hands on her apron. "What's this?" she asked, taking the invitation from her daughter, her green eyes sparkling as she looked from the paper to Ada.

"I have decided to host a ladies' tea twice a month."

Her friend's curiosity dimpled into a smile. "Who's invited?"

"Why you, Janey, and William, of course?" Ada shifted a gurgling Rosemary in her arms. "As well as myself and Rosie."

"What'll we do at somethin' as fancy as a ladies' tea?" Minnie dropped a mock curtsy that made both Ada and Janey laugh.

Ada felt a twinge of embarrassment. It wasn't as though she and Minnie didn't regularly visit with each other or take tea together. But she was hoping to do something out of the ordinary, something special to look forward to during the long winter hours.

"I had the idea to do teatime as I would if I were at Stonefield." By now, Minnie knew all about Ada's life before London. "I could teach Janey the proper way to pour and how to converse for hours on any number of tedious topics." She grinned at Minnie's daughter, who giggled again.

"Sounds right lovely," Minnie said. "'Specially on a dreary day like this one."

"My thoughts precisely. The three of you will come, then?"

Her friend nodded. "As soon as William wakes." Minnie added as she started to turn away, "I'll even bring me shortbread. If'n that's proper at a ladies' tea."

"Oh, it is more than proper," Ada called back. "It is a necessity."

Her friend's laughter lingered merrily in her ears as Ada exited the flat with Rosemary on her hip. Anticipation for their special teatime and gratitude for Minnie's willingness to join infused her with light and cheer and helped chase away some of the wintry dimness both without and within.

Chapter 7

April 1912

"THERE, THERE, PET," Ada soothed as she scooped up Rosemary from off the floor. The baby had toppled over in her attempt at walking and was now crying.

Smoothing back her daughter's dark curls, she handed Rosemary a spoon to play with. Her efforts at making bread were getting much closer to matching Minnie's loaves of perfection, but it was never an easy task with a nine-month-old underfoot.

"No wonder Mother employed an entourage of servants to help care for me."

Of course, Ada's mother hadn't been using her time alone to make bread, scrub nappies, or figure out how to stretch her pennies. But Ada wouldn't have it any other way. She was fulfilling her dream of building a loving, vibrant home—far different than the aloof, often lonely one she'd known back in Yorkshire.

The last few months, she'd even begun secretly repeating Ned's oft-used phrase of gratitude from his mealtime prayers—*Thank thee, Lord, for our bounteous blessings.*

Wouldn't he be surprised to know that? She wasn't quite ready to tell him yet, afraid her seedling of faith was still too fragile, especially in comparison with her husband's greater, stronger faith.

Setting her daughter back down on the floor, Ada kneaded the bread dough. Rosemary had stopped fussing over her tumble and was now gnawing away on the spoon.

"I believe Minnie is right," Ada said with a laugh. "You must have a new tooth."

It would explain the extra fussiness today and last night, which had kept Ada up for several hours. She brushed a strand of hair from her eyes with the back of her hand. When Rosemary napped later, perhaps she'd attempt to lie down as well.

When the dough had been fully kneaded, she set it inside two bread tins to rise. A knock at the door followed by a "'Ello, Ada" reached her in the kitchen.

"Afternoon, Minnie," Ada called back. "I'm making bread."

A moment later Minnie appeared, her burgeoning stomach leading the way. The birth of her friend's third child was drawing ever nearer. Five-year-old Janey followed behind Minnie, holding two-year-old William's hand.

"You aren't ready," Janey said, her expression changing from excited to crestfallen.

"Ready?" Ada shot Minnie a questioning look. Had she forgotten some other task or errand besides the bread?

Janey tugged William farther into the room. "It's ladies' teatime."

"Is it?" Ada shook her head at her own forgetfulness. Rosemary's teething had clearly taken a greater toll on her than just her physical strength. Apparently, it had meddled with her memory, too.

The girl cocked her head. "Mummy thought we'd do it today—"

"'Cause today is the day we do it," Minnie finished as she bustled forward, a covered plate in her hand. "Shall I put the kettle on?"

Ada eyed the mother and daughter in confusion, but she couldn't riddle out what was going on. "Yes, if you would, Minnie." She removed her floured apron, draped it over the table, and rolled down her sleeves. "Janey, if you'll see to Rosie, I will set the table in the parlor."

Her daughter had already started toddling toward Janey, whom she adored. Smiling, the girl picked up Rosemary. The baby promptly began babbling.

"Come with me, William," Ada said, taking the boy's hand in hers. She led him into the parlor, where she pulled some of her childhood books from the shelf and found the spools of thread he liked to play with as well.

When the boy was occupied, Ada removed the lace shawl from the trunk and draped it over the lid. Then she positioned the armchair closer to their makeshift table.

Minnie brought in one of the hard-back chairs from the kitchen.

"I ought to be doing that for you," Ada protested. "Why don't you sit in the chair of honor today?" She waved to the armchair, but Minnie was already shaking her head.

"I won't be climbin' outta there if'n I sit in that." She positioned the kitchen chair on the opposite end of the trunk. "This one'll do me fine." She sank into the chair with a contented sigh.

Ada went to the kitchen to gather up the teacups and saucers. She placed them and Minnie's plate of shortbread onto a tray, then carried it into the parlor. Janey trailed behind her with Rosemary in tow. She expected Janey to take the armchair, as the girl often did, but Minnie's daughter sat on the sofa instead, Rosemary on her lap.

"You may have the chair of honor, Janey." Ada set the tray on the trunk. "Your mum refuses her turn."

The girl shrugged. "You outta have it, Mrs. Henley. On account of it bein' . . ." A silencing look from her mother had Janey closing her mouth.

Ada placed her hands on her hips, an action she'd adopted from Minnie. "What are you two conspiring?"

"Not a thing." Minnie smiled innocently. "Is that the kettle I 'ear 'issin'?"

Throwing her friend another skeptical glance, which only made Minnie laugh, Ada returned to the kitchen. When the tea was ready, she carried the pot into the parlor and placed it beside the shortbread.

"Ladies' teatime has officially begun," she announced.

Before she could sit in the armchair, another knock sounded at the door. Ada glanced at Minnie in confusion. "Do you know who that might be?"

Minnie began pouring the tea since Janey still held Rosemary. She didn't look up as she remarked, "Couldn't say."

Perplexed, Ada moved to the hall and opened the door. Her husband stood on the other side, grinning. "Ned? Whatever are you doing here at this hour?" Sudden worry tightened her stomach. Had he been trying to protect her from more bad news? "Did they let you go?"

"No, love. Nothing like that." He stepped forward and kissed her cheek as if he were coming home for supper. "I had permission to leave the shop for a bit so I could wait for the train."

Ada frowned. "The train? I'm afraid you're not making any sense."

"Then perhaps this'll help." He stepped back and

motioned toward the bottom of the stairs. An older woman in a beautiful spring hat and a lace-covered gown stood there, her gloved hand gripping the wooden banister.

"Gran?" Ada's eyes widened in shock as she watched Ned assist her grandmother up the steps and into the flat. The rustle of silk and the scent of rosewater encompassed Ada as her grandmother embraced her.

"Happy birthday, my dearest Ada," Lucille murmured in a voice choked with emotion.

Ada stepped back, still unable to believe her grandmother stood before her. "I entirely forgot that it's my birthday." She threw a glance at the parlor and laughed. "That explains why the two of them wished to have teatime today."

"I asked Minnie to help with my surprise," Ned said with a grin.

"And a wonderful surprise it is, indeed. Thank you, Ned." Ada kissed her husband squarely on the lips, despite having an audience, then she looped her arm through Lucille's. "Come, Gran." She led her grandmother through the kitchen and into the parlor, Ned following behind them.

"Allow me to introduce my scheming yet dearest friend, Minnie O'Reilly," Ada said, waving to Minnie.

Despite her pregnant belly, Minnie managed to stand and drop a slight curtsy. "Pleased to meet you, ma'am."

"The pleasure is all mine, Mrs. O'Reilly," Lucille intoned with obvious sincerity. "Ada speaks quite highly of you and your family in her letters."

Minnie blushed, her cheeks matching her hair, but Ada could tell how much the compliment meant, particularly since it came from a fine society lady like her grandmother. Her friend introduced Lucille to Janey and William before Minnie took her seat again.

"Is this my darling great-grandbaby?" Lucille held out her hands to Rosemary.

Ada lifted her daughter from Janey's lap and carried her to Lucille. "Gran, may I present Rosemary Henley?"

Lucille took the child into her arms and fingered one of her dark curls. "Dear little Rosemary. You are the very image of your mother as a baby."

"Yes, but the curls and blue eyes are Ned's," Ada said proudly as she smiled at her husband.

Her grandmother settled into the armchair with Rosemary on her knee. "Shall we get to know one another, sweet one?"

Once Ada had collected another teacup, Minnie finished pouring the tea with all the poise of a duchess. Ada left hers untouched for the moment. Instead, she stood hand in hand with Ned, content to simply watch the happy scene. Nearly all of the people she loved were right here in this room.

"Are you happy, Ada?" Ned asked quietly as he lifted her hand to his lips and kissed her knuckles. She understood he was talking about much more than his surprise for her birthday.

"Quite happy."

She nestled against his side so she could rest her head on his shoulder. Her heart felt so full, she wasn't sure she could put the feelings into words. But she would try.

"Years from now," she whispered to him, "when Rosie is all grown up, and you and I are grandparents ourselves, I shall remember this day as one of the happiest of my life."

August 1914

Ada turned her chin upward so she could feel the

intermittent sunshine from beneath the brim of her hat. The sun might be weak where it peered through the clouds, but it was there nonetheless. The warm weather, combined with the extended bank holiday, meant the parkland in the middle of the houses and tenement buildings was far from empty.

Ned sat beside her, while three-year-old Rosemary chased after William and Janey in a game of their own making. Minnie and her husband, Thomas, were seated nearby. Their younger son, Alroy, kept plucking up the grass and trying to eat it, despite his mother's attempts to stop him.

The city had now been her and Ned's home for more than four years. On days like this one, there was no other place she'd rather be. Her life felt abundant with love, friendship, and hope.

"One-day holidays will feel much too short after experiencing four glorious days this week," she said, turning to her husband.

He smiled. "I feel as if I'm living like a gentleman."

"Only somehow, they seem to require holidays, too." They exchanged a laugh.

"It 'as been nice," Minnie agreed, "if just to pretend for a bit that we aren't at war."

At war. Despite what Ned had shared with Ada about the high tensions in Europe the past few weeks and the likelihood of Britain entering the conflict, the reality of it wouldn't stick within her mind. To her, war was something distant and intangible—an event from the past.

Still, a feeling of foreboding had been niggling at her all summer. Ada wasn't sure if it was all the talk about possibly going to war, but she sensed a pivotal change coming, and she feared it. She'd tried her best to ignore the feeling, though some days, she was more successful than others. Having Ned home these past four days had helped. It was hard to fathom what was happening elsewhere in the world when her own small one was full of contentment and peace.

"I saw it comin' to this," Thomas said with a shake of his head. "And while I don't like Britain breathin' down the necks of me Irish mates back home, I also know she can't stand aside after Germany refused to leave Belgium alone."

Ned nodded in agreement. "I'm with you, Thomas. Will you enlist, then?"

"Can't say I haven't thought of it, but the men at work are sayin' we're needed more at the motor factory than we are on a battlefield." He shifted on the grass to look curiously at Ned. "What about you? Are you enlistin'?"

Ada nearly laughed aloud at the absurdity. Ned was no soldier. Why would he enter the conflict? Besides, she thought with a sudden shiver, she could never bear living apart as they had before being married.

"I've considered it," Ned said, casting a hesitant glance at Ada. "But I haven't decided one way or the other."

She barely managed to keep herself from gaping at him. He'd thought about enlisting? Without talking to her? The ominous feeling in the pit of her stomach flared to life, bringing with it icy panic. He wouldn't leave her and Rosemary—he couldn't.

Rising to her feet, she addressed Ned without looking at him. "I believe I'll begin preparing supper. You and Rosemary come when you're finished here."

"See you tomorrow, Ada," Minnie said.

She nodded in response. Not even the look of compassion on her friend's face brought her comfort at the moment. She made it as far as the sidewalk before Ned caught up with her.

"Ada . . ." His cajoling tone angered her.

Turning to face him, she folded her arms against the

dread that threatened to consume her. "You promised, Ned. We both did—that we would work together. How is enlisting doing that?"

"I've only thought about it. I wouldn't go and enlist without talking to you."

She looked away. "You should have told me straightaway that you were considering it." She wasn't sure which hurt worse—that he'd been thinking about it at all or that she'd found out at the same time as their good friends.

"I know, love," he said after a moment, his chin low. "I'm sorry I didn't."

"Why consider it at all? You don't have to fight. At least, not yet." Hopefully, he never would.

"I have to protect you and Rosie." He reached out and took her hand in his. "To protect our way of life here."

"But we are speaking of war, Ned." She didn't bother to disguise the pleading in her tone. "I don't want to have to say goodbye; I don't want you gone."

"I don't wish to go," he admitted in a low voice. His next words sent another shudder through her. "But if it's right, Ada, I have to."

When he pulled her to him, she went. She shut her eyes and leaned into his touch. Was there anything she could say to persuade him differently? And if she did, was she breaking their promise to work together?

For the first time in their marriage, Ada suddenly understood what Ned had felt whenever he'd longed to protect her from something. That's what she wished to do in this moment—to protect him and herself.

"Go on, enjoy your last evening of holiday," she managed to say as she stepped back. "I'll have supper ready soon."

He studied her with concern. "You certain?"

"Yes." Tears rose into her throat, but she willed them back with a weak smile.

Giving her hand a squeeze, he turned back toward the grass. Ada headed for the flat at a brisk walk. She usually appreciated her time in the kitchen, her hands busy with the work they now knew so well, her mind free to think and ponder. But tonight, she wanted to silence her troubled thoughts and the awful premonition growing inside her that whispered this was only the beginning.

CHAPTER 8

RAINDROPS DRUMMED AGAINST the bedroom window. The sound mingled with Rosemary's soft snores from her small bed in the corner. However, neither noise had kept Ada awake this long. She lay nestled beneath Ned's arm, her hand resting against the front of his nightshirt. Through her palm, she felt the solid rhythm of his heartbeat.

Ned had been a constant source of strength and comfort to her in her life. And now he was leaving.

"Still awake?" he asked drowsily.

Ada nodded, wishing the decision he'd shared with her that evening had been a bad dream. Four weeks had passed since the bank holiday, and Ned had been thinking and praying about his enlistment ever since. She'd almost convinced herself that his answer would be *no,* but the resolve in his blue eyes had grown more pronounced the last few days. That had been as much an answer as his words tonight.

Ned brushed the hair off her forehead and pressed a kiss to her skin. The gesture usually prompted hope inside her, but in this moment, it only elicited stinging tears.

"It'll be fine, Ada." He lifted her chin. "I won't be shipped off right away."

"Can you wait a little longer?"

He tightened his embrace. "Not anymore, love. Not when Belgian citizens have been slaughtered."

She wanted to argue further, to find some way to make him stay and keep him safe. But her heart wouldn't allow it. How could she refuse to let him go when mothers not so unlike herself had already lost children, homes, and their own way of life?

If only his work at the print shop would help the war effort as Thomas's did. Minnie's husband had been right—he was needed more here. Ada hadn't been successful at fully squelching the envy she felt for him and Minnie.

"Mr. Silas promised me my position when I return." Ned twisted on his side to face her. "He said he'd look in on you and Rosie now and then, too."

Ada ran her fingers over the planes of his lips and the outline of his strong chin. How could she bear to be apart? She'd naively believed those three weeks she'd been away from him in Scotland had been hard. This time would be far worse. She had no way of knowing how long Ned would be gone or when he would come back to them.

"The two of you could go live with my mum," he said. "Then you'd not be on your own."

She knew Maud would gladly take them in, but Ada wasn't sure she could manage living in her mother-in-law's cottage, both of them anxious for word from Ned. Besides, Maud lived much too close to Stonefield Hall. Ada had made tentative peace with her parents' silence, especially after her decision not to write them anymore. But she didn't relish the thought of being in such close proximity as she awaited the return of her husband, whom they'd never accepted.

"I should like to stay here," she admitted, feeling the truthfulness of her statement as she voiced it. "Not having Minnie close by is something I cannot imagine."

The plucky redhead had become the sister Ada never had. She didn't want to face the difficult task of having her husband fighting as a soldier without Minnie nearby.

Ned kissed her fingertips. "I'm glad you'll still have Minnie and Thomas. I'll worry far less about you and Rosie knowing someone's there, if you have a need."

Quiet settled over them again, save for the rain and Rosemary's breathing. Ada tried to relax her mind in order to sleep, but dark thoughts threatened again. "Ned?"

"Hmm?"

"What if . . ." She pressed her lips together as the tears resurfaced, along with the now-familiar sense of foreboding. "You promise you will come back to us?"

Ned studied her a moment, then sat up. "I've something to read to you."

She willed back the tears and slid out of bed, as curious as she was relieved for a distraction. After ensuring their daughter still slept, Ada joined Ned in the parlor. He turned on the light, picked up his Bible from the shelf, and took a seat in the armchair.

"Come," he said, reaching out and gently pulling her onto his lap. Ada preferred no other spot.

When she was situated, he opened the Bible. "I read this verse the other day." It wasn't the first time he'd shared scriptures with her, either in answer to a question she had or to share something he liked.

Ada rested her head on his shoulder as he began to read in a deep voice, "'Be strong and of a good courage; be not afraid, neither be thou dismayed: for the Lord thy God is with thee whithersoever thou goest.'"

"Read it again, please," she murmured, and Ned obliged her request.

She liked the hopefulness in the words. But were they true?

"Do you believe that?" She fingered the lapel of his pajamas. "That God is truly with us—with you and me—wherever we go?"

He rubbed his thumb across her cheek. "I do. He'll be with me and with you, and Rosie, too." Nudging her chin upward, he gazed tenderly at her. "And you, love? Do you believe it?"

She stared down at the open Bible, searching her heart for the answer. They took turns praying at mealtimes now, and sometimes, Ada found herself thinking prayers to God during the course of the day. But did she truly believe He was with her, that He knew and cared about her?

"I wish to believe it. But is that enough? I feel so childlike in matters of faith." Ada blew out a soft sigh. "You and Minnie are far more knowledgeable than I."

Ned gathered her to him again. "Jesus asked us that we all become like a little child."

"How so?"

He appeared to ponder that. "How does Rosie feel toward us as her mum and dad?"

"She loves us."

"Trusts us, too?"

Ada nodded.

"Are we angry she knows less than you and me? Or less than, say, Janey or William?"

"Of course not," Ada said, understanding flooding her thoughts. "We know eventually she will learn all that she must as we continue to teach her and she continues to trust us."

She sensed Ned's smile. "Exactly. God feels the same. He doesn't compare you to anyone else. He knows you weren't taught to trust or love Him as were Minnie and I. But that doesn't mean He is any less aware of you or loves you less, Ada. You've always been and always will be His daughter."

Warmth spread through her at his words. She might have lost contact with her earthly father, but she still had a Heavenly One who knew and loved her. And God would not abandon her.

"Can you sleep now?" Ned asked, pressing his forehead to hers.

The question yanked Ada back to reality, eroding some of her peace. "I suppose so."

"I want to promise I'll come back." His tone held more grimness than she'd ever heard. "But you know I can't. I can promise never to stop loving you and to remember you and Rosie every day."

She sat back so she could hold his face between her palms. "I promise you the same."

When she kissed him, she held nothing back, pouring all of her fears and wishes into the kiss. Ned responded with equal fervor, until it seemed as if nothing existed outside of them and the flat. And Ada hoped it would be that way again one day soon.

"Mummy, my legs are tired," Rosemary complained, pulling back against Ada's hand. "Can't you carry me?"

Fighting impatience, Ada stopped walking and crouched beside her daughter. "You are too big to carry, pet. I know your legs are tired, but we've run out of meat, and we need to walk to the butcher shop to purchase more." She stood, trying to think of something to take Rosemary's mind off the walk ahead. "Would you care to give the boy our coin in exchange for a newspaper?"

"Oh, yes, Mummy." Rosemary allowed Ada to guide her forward, happy once again.

But Ada felt a twinge of guilt. While handing over the coin might be enjoyable to her daughter, the possibility of what lay inside the newspaper had the potential to obliterate their happiness.

Ever since Ned had left for France the month before, Ada had purchased as many newspapers as she could afford to check the casualty lists. Minnie didn't believe it healthy or hopeful to peruse them so often, but Ada wouldn't be dissuaded. In some inexplicable way, she felt more in control of her fears when she checked to see that Ned's name wasn't listed than when she didn't.

"There he is, Mummy." Rosemary pointed at the newsboy, who was shouting, "Paper, paper. News, news."

Ada pulled a coin from her purse, then watched as Rosemary hurried up to the boy and presented him with the money. In return, he thrust a paper into her small hand. Ada took it from her daughter. The names of places she'd never heard of before this year—Marne, Aisne, and Antwerp—filled the newsprint and were mentioned on nearly every street in London these days.

She opened the paper to the casualty lists, her heart leaping into her throat as it always did. Ada quickly read through the *H* names. When she didn't see "Henley" listed, she let herself relax, though she read through the names once more, just to be certain.

Closing the paper, she tucked it under her arm and steered Rosemary down the street. "We will be at the butcher shop soon."

Was she nurturing her newly sprouted faith by checking the papers like this? The question poked at her, disrupting the relative calm she'd felt at not finding Ned's name among the casualties. Ada led the prayers at mealtimes now, and she'd begun praying every night for Ned's safety as well. Yet her uncertainty and helplessness about the future wouldn't leave her alone.

"Mummy?" Rosemary tugged on Ada's hand a second time, her voice concerned.

She pushed her distressing thoughts aside. "The shop is right there, pet."

"But, Mummy. Look there . . ."

"I understand you're tired, pet," she said, her impatience bleeding into her voice. "But all we have to do is cross the street, and we will—"

The shattering of glass pierced the air and cut off the rest of her words. Rosemary gave a frightened yelp. "What are they doing, Mummy?"

Ada stopped short as her gaze went to the butcher's shop across the street. A group had formed in front of the building, where the front window now stood jagged and broken. The door had been bashed in as well. As she watched, horrified, several men and a woman swarmed the shop before exiting with armfuls of meat.

"What happened to the window?" Rosemary asked.

"It-it's broken, pet."

Another woman stood watching the scene, too, one hand resting protectively against her collar. Ada walked toward her. "Do you know what's happened at the butcher shop?"

"Isn't just them." The woman shook her head. "The German-owned bakery round the corner was also sacked and looted."

Her shock mounting, Ada glanced at the meat shop once more. The place appeared to have been stripped of its wares in a matter of minutes.

"It's them refugees from Antwerp what started the trouble, though I doubt they meant to." The woman turned toward Ada. "Lots of people round here are angry at Germany for what they done. Some of them refugees only have the clothes on their backs."

"Surely, the butcher is not responsible..."

The woman shrugged. "If'n you're angry or afraid, you aren't stoppin' to think who's responsible, now are you?"

"Mummy, are we still going to buy our meat?"

Ada looked down at Rosemary. "Not from here, pet. We'll have to go elsewhere." Before her daughter could let out another groan of protest, she changed her mind. She felt suddenly as tired as Rosemary at that moment. "On second thought, we can wait to find meat another day. I believe we'll go home instead."

As she led her daughter away from the dreadful scene, Ada couldn't help a backward glance. Where was the German family who owned the shop? Had they escaped unharmed? While she fostered some anger toward Germany herself, she liked to think she knew better than to take her resentment out on innocent people who did not even live in their native country any longer. She tightened her grip on Rosemary's hand and quickened her steps, anxious to return to the safety of their flat.

"Were they angry?" Rosemary's blue eyes, so like Ned's, gazed innocently up at Ada. "The people who broke the window and took the meat?"

"Yes, Rosie. They were angry and scared. However, that does not make it right to break into another person's shop and take what is not theirs."

Rosemary's small mouth twisted into a perplexed frown. "Why were they scared?"

Ada paused. She wanted to give her daughter a satisfactory answer, but without frightening her. "Everyone feels scared now and then, pet. The trick is not to allow our fears to take charge of us."

"Do you feel scared, Mummy?"

She swallowed hard. Her guilt over buying the paper out of fear stung her as much as her daughter's question. "Sometimes."

"How come?" Rosemary asked, cocking her head.

What would Ned say? "Even mummies and daddies can forget that when things are frightening or confusing, God is still with us."

"And that helps you not feel scared." Her daughter's tone was matter-of-fact and full of trust.

When I remember that truth, pet, she thought.

But Ada hadn't been remembering. Not really. She'd been praying, but in some ways, she was acting as much out of fear as the people who'd looted the butcher shop. Thankfully, God had given her a reminder through Rosemary's innocence. After all, even Ada was supposed to become like a little child.

Stopping, she bent down to be at eye level with Rosemary. In Ned's absence, it was her responsibility to be an example of faith to their daughter. Which meant no more buying newspapers to check the casualty lists. Even as she made the decision, her heart hammered with apprehension. Yet she sensed a measure of calm, too.

"Rosie, what if you said the prayer for supper tonight, to bless the food and to bless Daddy? Would you like that?"

Her blue eyes widened as she nodded. "Uh-huh."

"Wonderful."

She gave her daughter a hug, then stood. It was past time to teach her daughter more about God and faith than just mealtime prayers. Ada might not know as much as her husband or Minnie, but she had a desire to learn—as Rosemary did—and surely, that was enough for now.

Chapter 9

July 1915

STACKS OF PAPER consumed Ada's days and filled her dreams at night, but she was grateful for her employment. It helped her feel closer to Ned. They were both doing their bit for the war effort—she in London and he in France.

Ada removed another section from the large railway ledger in front of her and tossed it into the waist-high pile beside the table. The old paper would be sorted, stored, and eventually reused. Unlike a position at one of London's munitions factories, her work at the paper warehouse was safe and required little thought or hard labor, which meant plenty of opportunities to visit with her fellow female workers.

The extra income was welcome, too, supplementing Ned's separation allowance. A little of Ada's wages went to her mother-in-law in Yorkshire, and despite Minnie's protests, a little went to the O'Reillys each month in exchange for watching Rosemary.

"Where do you s'pose Belinda is?" Ada's friend Lillie asked, looking up from the ledger she was dismantling.

Ada glanced around at the others working nearby. "I don't know."

Belinda Kilpatrick was typically the first one in line outside the warehouse each morning. Yet Ada suddenly recalled with a flicker of concern that her friend hadn't been in her usual spot. Hopefully, their supervisor wouldn't notice her absence.

Her hopes plummeted when the man, balding and in his late forties, approached her and Lillie a few minutes later, a scowl on his round face. "You seen Mrs. Kilpatrick? She's late." He used a cloth riddled with smudges to wipe his forehead. "If she don't want her position no more, I can fill it 'fore noon."

"She will be here," Ada said with feigned confidence. While she didn't know Belinda as well as she did Minnie, the woman had a husband serving in France. That was reason enough to defend her.

Belinda was several years older than Ada and had been unable to have children before her husband left for the war. She'd confided that she'd taken this job to fill her daytime hours with something other than fretting over her husband's well-being. Ada could relate.

Though she'd vanquished most of the fear she'd felt that first month after Ned had left, there were days she still struggled. So when Thomas had mentioned openings for women at the paper warehouse, she'd immediately applied. The companionship and employment, coupled with her efforts to nurture her budding faith and share it with Rosemary, had proven to be a fairly sufficient antidote for her worries.

"She best be here," their supervisor mumbled as he stalked away.

Ada and Lillie worked in silence for a while longer before the other woman declared in a loud whisper, "It's Belinda."

Lifting her chin, Ada watched as Belinda walked toward them. Her shoulders were stooped, and her face was devoid of color. Ada reached out and took the woman by the elbow. "Belinda, whatever's the matter?"

"I . . ." Belinda licked her lips, her gaze darting back and forth. "I wouldn't have been late, but . . ." She lifted her hand to show Ada the piece of paper she held.

Dread curdled inside Ada's stomach at the sight of the telegram from the War Office. Belinda's thumb covered some of the words, but Ada could read the worst of them—*killed in action* and *deepest sympathy.*

"Oh, Belinda. I'm so very sorry."

The woman gave a hollow laugh. "Is this what we do here?" Her gray eyes shone wild with grief. "Sort through all this blasted paper so that they can make this?" She waved the telegram. "Is that what we do?" she repeated, her voice catching on a sob.

Ada swallowed hard. "Why not sit for a few moments?" It wouldn't help matters if the supervisor overheard Belinda's grieving rant.

"No." Belinda shook her head. "I hate paper. I hate it!" She rushed to the nearest pile and pushed it over. The mountain of pages cascaded like a waterfall across the warehouse floor. "I won't be a part of this madness any longer." She was fully sobbing now.

The looks of pity from the other women compelled Ada to take action. She took Belinda by the arm and steered her around the table, away from the stares of their friends and the ever-watchful gaze of their ill-tempered supervisor. When they reached a sturdier pile of paper, Ada helped Belinda sit on top of the mound.

"Breathe for bit," Ada directed as she knelt in front of Belinda.

Belinda gulped in a shaky breath. "I can't live without him, Ada, I can't."

How many times had she thought this same sentiment in her darker moments of what-if? But it would do Belinda no good for Ada to share that, not when the unthinkable had become her friend's reality.

"I know how badly it can hurt." While her husband hadn't been killed, Ada could understand the pain of loss—both from her miscarriage and her parents' rejection. "Sometimes, you cannot even see straight for the ache inside your heart."

After a minute or two, Belinda's sobs eased to sniffles. "What'll I do?" She wiped at her wet cheeks, her gaze pleading.

What could Ada say that might help? Snatches of memory, of things Ned had shared with her, resurfaced in her thoughts.

"Do you believe there is a God, Belinda?"

Her friend hesitated a moment, then dipped her chin in a nod.

"Then turn to Him, because He believes in you, too," Ada said, feeling the conviction of the words as she voiced them. "He loves you. You can ask Him for help, and He'll provide it."

She rose to her feet, and Belinda did the same. Some of the whiteness had left the woman's face, and her gaze no longer appeared as harried.

"Do you wish to spend the rest of the day at home?" Not that their supervisor would allow it, but Ada would work twice as hard if it meant her friend could have another day to move through her grief.

Belinda shook her head. "No. I can work." She slipped the telegram inside the pocket of her skirt. "Thank you, Ada."

Nodding, Ada returned to her table as some of the other

women approached Belinda. A somber mood settled over the entire group when the grieving widow finally joined them in righting the tumbled pile and pulling apart the ledgers.

Ada threw herself into her work, eager to keep her hands busy. Her mind was another matter. She'd felt the truthfulness of what she had told Belinda about God. But this was also the first time someone she knew had lost a soldier to the war. It was dreadful and sobering. And she couldn't help hoping and praying as she worked that somehow, she might escape this type of loss. Because, unlike the other losses in her life, she felt certain she could not weather this one.

"We must go, Rosie, or I shall be late," Ada called from where she stood in the hallway.

Rosemary emerged from the bedroom, her shoes dangling from her hand instead of on her feet. "But I don't want to go," she whined. "It isn't any fun without William there."

Exhaling through her nose and hoping she would still be on time to the warehouse, Ada crossed the room and gently seated her daughter on the kitchen floor. "I know you don't enjoy it there without William, pet." He and Rosie were the best of friends. "However, next year, you will be at school with him and Janey. That will be lovely, right?"

"Yes," Rosemary said with a sigh.

Ada helped her with her shoes, then smoothed back Rosemary's unruly curls from her forehead. "All ready now?"

"Yes, Mummy." Climbing to her feet, she placed her small hand inside Ada's larger one. "Minnie says I'm getting all growed up, and I can watch Alroy and Baby Molly all by myself when she makes lunch."

"That is very grown up indeed." Ada smiled as she led Rosemary out the door and down the stairs. She couldn't believe her daughter was already four years old.

Where has the time gone? she wondered with a shake of her head. Rosemary had changed from a toddler to a little girl this last year, and Ada felt a pang of regret that Ned had missed the transformation.

She did her best to keep him apprised of her job and their daughter, but letters were a poor substitute for being together. She longed to touch his face and hold him in her arms, longed to see Ned toss Rosemary up in the air as he used to, all three of them laughing. Hopefully, he'd be granted leave soon.

Swallowing her intense feelings of missing him, Ada guided Rosemary into the neighboring building and knocked on Minnie's door. Her friend answered a few moments later, holding Baby Molly.

"Good morning," Ada said, running a gloved finger over Molly's plump cheek.

The baby gave her a toothless smile in return. The sight of it brought as much delight as it did pain. Ada wished she might have had another child before Ned had left for France, but it hadn't worked out that way.

"I apologize for being late . . ." Her words ran out when she noticed Minnie's red-rimmed eyes. Something was wrong. "Rosie, why don't you find Alroy and see if he wishes to play a game with you?"

Taking Molly into her arms, Ada ushered Minnie into the kitchen. "Whatever is the matter?"

"It's downright awful, Ada." Minnie sank into a chair, stifling a sob with her hand. "'E's gone and done it."

Alarm made her heart throb faster. In the five years she'd known Minnie, Ada had never seen her in such a state. "Who has gone and done what?"

"Thomas. 'E went to enlist this morning." Minnie dabbed at her eyes with the corner of her apron. "I begged 'im not to go, but 'e said 'e 'ad to."

Shocked, Ada lowered herself into the adjacent chair, then bounced Molly on her knees. "But he's already doing war work. He has the badge and certificate to prove it."

Minnie shook her head. "I know. But 'e sees them women 'anding out their white feathers of shame and feels it inside 'imself. Thinkin' people are still judging 'im 'cause 'e's not wearing a soldier's kit."

"Oh, Minnie." Ada placed her hand over her friend's where it lay limp on top of the table. Empathy brought the blur of tears to her own eyes. She'd once envied Minnie that her husband hadn't gone to fight, but now she wished Thomas wasn't leaving.

"I don't what I'll do, Ada." Her question mirrored Belinda's from two months ago. Minnie's expression crumbled anew as her gaze strayed to the baby. "I've got four wee ones. The separation money will 'elp, but I'm not sure I can get a job like you to cover anything more."

"Then it's a good thing you are due for a pay raise for watching Rosie."

Minnie frowned, but before she could protest, Ada rushed on. "We must help each other, Minnie." She squeezed her hand firmly, determination welling up anew inside her. "Whatever comes, we will make it through together—with God to help us. Fair enough?"

A strangled laugh escaped Minnie's lips, followed by a nod of agreement. "Fair enough." She reached for Molly. "Thank you."

"You're quite welcome." She stood. "Heaven only knows how much you have helped me. I am grateful for the chance to finally return the favor."

Minnie arched an eyebrow. "Who says you 'aven't already been 'elping me all these years?" She trailed Ada to the kitchen doorway. "You've been a good friend and example."

"Example of what?" Ada asked with a self-deprecating chuckle. She'd learned so much from Minnie—she couldn't think of what she'd shared in return.

"Of strength, compassion, courage." Minnie bumped her shoulder. "I like watchin' you come to know God, too. Makes me want to be more earnest like that."

Ada could think of no greater compliment. Growing up, success had meant owning the most fashionable clothes or the largest estate. That was the reason she'd hoped to teach and cultivate within her children different values than those she'd known. Hearing Minnie's praise in this moment, she felt closer to having the sort of home, of being the sort of person, she'd dreamt of for so long.

Unlike in Scotland before she and Ned had married, Ada was the one rapidly moving through the train station today. She paused beside a group of soldiers, their uniforms pockmarked with dried mud. When she didn't see the familiar face she sought, she hurried on. Thankfully, she'd left Rosemary with Minnie, which meant Ada didn't have to slow her pace to match her daughter's shorter strides.

Her heart leapt with anticipation as she searched the faces of a trio of soldiers. But Ned wasn't with them. She kept walking, winding her way quickly around the scenes of homecoming and farewell all around her.

"Ada!"

She stopped at the sound of his voice from behind. Had

she strode right past him? Whirling, she looked around, her pulse threading faster. There he was, standing to one side, near the train. He was skinnier than she'd ever seen him, his blue eyes less bright. But it was Ned!

His expression lit with relief and longing, then he strode forward and captured her in his arms. Ada held him tightly, laughing and sobbing at the *thrum-thrum* of his heartbeat beneath his jacket. "You are home at last."

"That I am, love." He kissed her lips hungrily. There were tears shining in his eyes when he eased back. "You're more beautiful than I remembered."

Blushing with pleasure, she cupped his thin face between her hands. The scruff of his jaw grazed her fingertips. She could hardly believe this wasn't a dream—they were here together.

"Rosie is beyond excited to see you. She is waiting for us at the O'Reillys'."

Instead of stooping to pick up his pack so they might leave, Ned remained in place. "I've missed you so, Ada." The intensity of his gaze renewed the frenzied rhythm of her heartbeat.

"I've missed you, too, darling. Can you believe an entire year has truly come and gone?"

A shadow passed over his handsome face, making her wonder what he'd seen and experienced in that time. While he knew nearly everything about her days, he'd shared so little about his own.

Then his eyes sparked with the warmth and kindness she'd seen the first time they'd talked. "I'm proud of you—of us. We managed, didn't we?" he said.

"Indeed, we did." She had to swallow hard as she added, "With help from God."

Ned appeared momentarily surprised at her words

before his mouth lifted in a grin. Embracing her again, he swung her around, making her laugh with dizzy pleasure. When he set her down, it was only to hold her close once more. Ada sensed what he didn't say aloud—that he didn't want to let her go. It was a feeling she understood perfectly. She, too, wished to hold him close forever.

Part 2

Chapter 10

France, May 1916

IT WAS THE smell of the soldiers that first hit Hugh Whittington each time he met with a group on reserve. However, the men took no notice of the terrible scent, one that stank of unwashed bodies, mud, and death. After the stench, it was the dogged perseverance of the soldiers that always struck him next.

The nearest he'd come thus far to the front lines were the various shelled-out villages he visited, like the one he'd been driven to tonight. Not that he feared being in harm's way. What he feared was the guilt that would surely overtake him if he witnessed up close what his brother and the other soldiers had faced—and continued to face—during the war.

His mother had been the one to suggest the trip to France. Wouldn't Hugh like to see how well the boots his factory turned out day after day were holding up through the war? He'd known the real reason behind her suggestion. Helena Whittington was worried about Harry, and this was a way for her to learn for certain if her youngest son was cracking on all right.

Hugh entered the shelled house where he'd been told he would find the soldiers. Candles and cigarettes pushed the shadows to the corners of the partially toppled walls. The men talked quietly or dozed, their equipment at the ready in the event they were called up to help.

The group's commanding officer shook Hugh's hand and introduced him to several of the soldiers seated near the door-less entryway. Hugh explained who he was—the maker of the boots they wore—and asked them what improvements could be made to the shoes.

As he made his way around the room, Hugh noticed a soldier in the corner staring down at a photograph he held between his hands. There was something familiar about the man's thin, bearded face.

Then the soldier glanced up. His eyes widened in shock at seeing Hugh at the same instant recognition flooded Hugh's thoughts.

"Ned Henley?" he exclaimed, hardly believing he'd stumbled across his former gamekeeper and Ada's husband.

Ned stood and shook Hugh's hand in a friendly grasp. "Hugh Whittington! What are you doing here?"

"I wished to see firsthand how our soldiers' boots are faring." He smiled as he added in a lower voice, "Although I shall freely confess to you that is but one reason I'm here. My mother wanted to ensure my brother Harry is fine."

The man's smile conveyed understanding. "Have you seen Harry, then?"

"Not yet, no. I've been told I shall tomorrow."

As usual, the thought of seeing his brother again elicited a mixture of emotion inside Hugh. He longed for it and feared it at the same time.

What sort of older, protecting brother was he to allow his younger brother to run off to fight without joining him? Hugh had attempted to convince himself again and again that he was needed in Yorkshire to run the factory. Yet he hoped that Harry might be as proud of him for staying behind as Hugh was of him for being a soldier.

"I can't tell you how good it is to see a familiar face." Ned grinned. "Have you seen my mum lately? Is she well?"

Hugh indicated that Ned should sit back down as he took a spot along the nearby wall for himself. "I looked in on her before I left, and she is in good health. How are Ada and your little girl?"

"They're well." Ned leaned his head back against the wall. "Ada's been working in a paper warehouse since last year. Seems to like it, too. She's taken well to life in London." The pride in his tone was unmistakable.

"I'm glad to hear it. And her parents? Have they come around?" It had troubled Hugh greatly that Charles and Victoria Thorne had refused to speak of Ada the past few years. Last he'd heard from his mother, Ada's parents had not bothered to write their daughter, either. But perhaps that had changed recently.

Ned frowned. "No, they haven't come round yet."

A pang of sadness and anger shot through him at Ned's answer. At least Ada sounded happy, in spite of her parents' actions.

"How are things at the factory?" Ned asked.

Hugh told him how they were turning out four hundred pairs of boots a day, then asked about Ned's time at the print shop. Soon, they were trading stories of Yorkshire and London. Some of Hugh's guilt eased with the camaraderie. Ned did not appear to condemn or judge Hugh for not fighting in France.

"Would you like me to take a letter to your mother?" It was a simple thing, but it was a way to help Ned nonetheless.

Hand-delivering a letter to Maud Henley would mean she would hear that much sooner from her son.

Ned's expression lit with enthusiasm. "That's a capital idea. Thank you."

"I shall let you write, then," Hugh said as he climbed to his feet, "while I speak with some of the others."

He finished making his way around the room, conversing with the soldiers about their boots. By the time he returned to Ned's corner, the man was on his feet and had two letters to give him.

"This one's for Ada," Ned explained. "Would you mind posting it when you get back?"

"Not at all." Hugh slipped both letters into his jacket pocket. His driver signaled him from the doorway. Unfortunately, it was time to go. "It was good to see you again, Henley."

"You, too." They shook hands once more. "Thank you for watching over my mum."

"It's the least I can do. We are praying for you and Harry and all of the others from Yorkshire."

Ned nodded. "Thank you for that, too."

"Take care, Henley."

"I will. Tell Harry hello from me."

Hugh smiled. "I shall pass along the greeting." He started to walk away, but Ned called after him.

"Whittington?"

He turned. "Yes?"

The man's face registered far more seriousness now than Hugh had ever seen there before. "Would you do something else for me?" At Hugh's nod, Ned continued. "If I don't return home . . ." He maintained a level gaze, though his eyes filled with momentary pain. "Will you promise to look after Ada and Rosemary for me?"

Hugh didn't need to pause to consider his answer; he knew it at once. "I give you my word, Henley."

"I'm much obliged." Some of his somberness faded. "You're a good man, Hugh Whittington. I wager God's got you right where He needs you."

Though the statement took Hugh aback, it still had the power to ease a bit of his shame, too. "I hope so."

He waved goodbye to Ned, who offered a wave in return, then Hugh followed his driver from the building. It had been more than coincidental that he'd run into Ned tonight. He felt certain God had orchestrated it—perhaps for both of them.

London, July 1916

The knock sounded different from Minnie's. It was heavier and more ominous, Ada remembered later. She wiped her hands on a towel and instructed Rosemary to continue reading at the table as she went to open the door.

A delivery boy, no older than thirteen, stood waiting, an envelope clutched in his hand. At the sight of it, Ada froze. Her eyes and heart knew exactly what the youth's presence and the telegram signified, but her head still protested. She'd had a letter from Ned only two days earlier, and he was due for leave again soon. News such as this could not come now.

"I've somethin' for Mrs. Henley."

She had to swallow hard to force an answer from her dry throat. "I am Mrs. Henley."

The young man extended the envelope toward her, though she didn't miss the pained look in his eyes. "My deepest sympathies, ma'am."

She could only manage a nod as she closed her trembling fingers around the envelope. The boy offered her one more sympathetic glance before he turned and headed down the stairs. Ada shut the door, her thoughts chaotic, her feelings numb. Ned might only be injured or missing in action. It might not be what she feared the most.

"Who was at the door, Mummy?" Rosemary called from the kitchen.

She cleared her throat. "It was about a . . . a letter."

"From Daddy?"

Ada sucked in a sharp breath at her daughter's innocent question. A prick of pain attempted to breach her shock, but she fought it back. She must first manage supper and putting Rosemary to bed.

"No, not this one, pet," Ada answered as she walked into the parlor and set the envelope face down on the trunk. "Shall we eat?"

Somehow, she managed to make conversation with her daughter through the meal and while they washed and dried the dishes afterward, though Rosemary had to ask more than once if Ada was listening. Numbness had wrapped itself tightly around her, making it difficult to concentrate on any one thing.

"What would you like to read tonight?" she asked with feigned cheerfulness when the kitchen had been set to rights and Rosemary had donned her long white nightgown.

"Your apron is still on." Rosemary giggled.

Ada looked down, not even remembering what dress she'd put on that morning. "So it is." She removed the apron, draped it over the vanity chair, and forced a quick smile. "Now I'm ready."

Rosemary surveyed her mother, her blue eyes unusually grave. "Is something wrong, Mummy?"

Everything, pet. But Ada couldn't say that.

"We'll be right enough." The words tasted more of lies than truth. "Will you select a story?"

As Rosemary left the room, Ada sank onto the bed, her hand splayed against the blanket. Would Ned ever lie here again beside her? Emotion raced up her throat, bitter and choking. She hurried to swallow it back as her daughter reentered the room with a book in hand.

Ada leaned against the headboard while Rosemary snuggled next to her, then she began to read aloud. It seemed to take longer than usual for her daughter to finally fall asleep. Ada didn't know whether to feel frustrated or relieved by that. Now nothing stood between her and the telegram in the parlor.

She scooped up Rosemary and placed her on the bed in the corner. Pulling the blankets over her daughter's sleeping from, Ada was bombarded with the first rush of tears. But she bit her lip, hard, to stay them a bit longer and slipped into the parlor.

Eyeing the envelope, she moved to the bookcase to put the bedtime story away. She straightened a few knickknacks as well. An intense weight pressed against her lungs and the backs of her eyes until she could hardly breathe. There was no sense avoiding the inevitable any longer.

She picked up the telegram and sat in the armchair—to her, it was still Ned's seat, even in his absence. Its solidness brought her a flicker of comfort. She broke the seal and removed the single sheet of paper, letting the envelope slip to the floor.

Killed in action.

They were the only words she saw, the only ones that mattered. And though they weren't entirely unexpected, they managed to hit her with the force of a locomotive.

Ada squelched the urge to crush the telegram in her fist and toss it into the rubbish bin. This was one of her last connections to Ned, so she forced herself to read every painful word of the short message.

There was mention of sympathy from the War Office, which brought a bitter laugh from her dry lips. They hadn't known Ned, hadn't loved him as she had, hadn't believed they'd have a long life together. The feeling of detachment cracked wide open at the latter thought, and with it, Ada's heart. A powerful ache filled her chest. How could her husband be gone for good?

"Oh, Ned," she whispered, as much in anger as in agony. "Why? Why?"

Tears burned her throat and eyes, insisting on release. Ada couldn't have held them back if she'd wanted. Pressing her fingers to her mouth to muffle her cries, she sobbed, the telegram strangled in her other hand. It wasn't supposed to be this way. Ned was supposed to live, to return to them for good. She didn't want to raise their daughter alone.

She remained in the chair until her sobs and her energy were both spent. Then she slipped to the floor, too shattered to sit upright any longer. She pressed her cheek to the rug, uncertain what to do. Should she remain in London, near the O'Reillys? After all, she had employment here. Or should she return to Stonefield Hall and attempt to reconcile with her parents?

No, she thought in answer as fresh anger stirred inside her. Her parents had never accepted Ned. If she went back now, it would almost be like he—and the life they'd created for themselves—had never existed.

She and Rosemary would remain in London.

Her next decision ought to be how to tell her daughter the news about Ned. Another ache knifed through Ada. She didn't wish to think about that just yet. The little girl had only a handful of memories of her father, and now there was no hope for more.

Why, God? She squeezed her eyes shut and swallowed back a wail. Her faith felt more fragile than it ever had before. *I can't bear this alone. Please, help me.*

She lay on the rug a long time, the tears drying on her face. Exhaustion filled her limbs, her mind, her heart. Would God answer her anguished prayer? Was He really with her, or were her own words of comfort to Belinda and Minnie not applicable to her?

After a minute, Ada climbed stiffly to her feet. She smoothed the wrinkles from the telegram and placed it inside Ned's Bible before moving toward the bedroom. She hoped sleep would come mercifully swift tonight.

CHAPTER 11

HUGH RUBBED HIS tired eyes, then attempted to focus once more on the order form he held in his hand. While overseeing the boot factory could be exhausting, especially these days, he was grateful to provide footwear to the men in the trenches and employment to their mothers, sisters, wives, and sweethearts at home. He now had far more female employees at the factory than men. And while the majority of them were far more talkative than their male counterparts, all of them had proven to be efficient workers.

The animation and quiet strength they brought to the factory reminded him of Ada Henley, working herself in London. A smile lifted one corner of his mouth as he recalled times from Ada's youth when she'd demonstrated a similar streak of independence. Was it really a surprise, then, that she'd married the man she'd wanted to, instead of allowing her parents to dictate her choice? Hugh admired her for that. Her and Ned both.

He thought back to his chance meeting with Ned in France two months earlier. The man's parting words—*I wager God has you right where He needs you*—had entered his thoughts over and over since then.

Hugh wanted to believe he was in the right place, doing what God wanted him to do here in Yorkshire. He'd made the choice at his father's death to assume responsibility for the factory—as the elder son should. A decision he hadn't felt right about renouncing, even after England had gone to war. Besides, unlike Harry, he'd never had aspirations to be a soldier. There were still moments, however, when he wondered if he'd rather be wearing the boots from his factory instead of making them.

Tossing the form onto his desk, he leaned back in his chair. He'd been devoting all of his time and energy to managing the factory as well as the estate for a long time now. But was such a contribution enough?

"Enough for who?" he murmured out loud, sniffing in amusement at talking to himself.

Were his efforts enough for his family? His country? His God?

A knock at his office door interrupted his introspection. Sitting forward, he called out, "Come."

His secretary, Mr. Bertrup, entered the room, looking apprehensive. "There's a delivery boy here to see you, sir. Says he has a telegram. Shall I send him in?"

A telegram? Hugh could think of only a handful of reasons he'd be receiving a telegram, and most of them meant unpleasant news. His chest squeezed with dread, but he forced himself to take a full breath.

"Thank you, Mr. Bertrup," he said with outer calm. "You may send him in."

One of the lads from the village slipped inside the office. He appeared as anxious as Hugh's secretary.

Hugh stood. "How may I help you, John? It is John, is it not?"

"Yes, sir." John approached the desk. "I 'ave a telegram for you, Mr. Whittington, sir."

The lad extended the envelope. Hugh took it, feeling the weight of its contents in spite of the envelope's lightness.

"I'm right sorry, sir." John's sorrowful expression conveyed how much he meant the words—they were not spoken tritely.

"I'm sorry, too." He studied the boy. "You have a rather beastly job at present."

John shrugged, but the look on his young face told a different story. "It pays..."

"But it's difficult, too," Hugh finished. After a moment, John lowered his chin in a nod. How many other boys throughout Britain were shouldering similar burdens, delivering vital but unwanted news? It was more grief and pain than boys this age should have to bear.

The lad shuffled backward. "I best be on my way, sir."

"Goodbye, then, John."

Hugh waited for the boy to exit his office before he sat down. He swallowed past his suddenly dry throat as he broke open the envelope and withdrew the telegram. The pounding of his heart seemed to stop altogether when he read the short message.

Harry had been killed in action.

Grief, sharp and cutting, speared his chest as Hugh dropped the telegram onto his cluttered desk. Never again in this life would he watch Harry bustle into his office, a ready grin on his brother's face and a teasing remark on his tongue. They would never share another laugh or confide their deepest thoughts to one another.

Resting his elbows on his desk, he pressed the palms of his hands against the tears in his eyes. If he'd been the one to go to war and Harry had stayed... He cut off the thought. Harry had never had any inclination to manage the boot factory.

Hugh would need to inform his mother and sisters of the news, as well as the young lady in the village who Harry had been sweet on before leaving for France. Fresh pain cut through him at having to share such shattering tidings with all of them, but especially his mother.

Harry was the youngest of the five Whittington children and a true joy in their mother's life. Hugh only hoped this news wouldn't kill her. The notion of bearing the weight of his family's grief, along with his own, left him feeling weary down to his bones.

He pushed back his chair and stood, anxious to get the dreadful task over sooner than later. Surely, he could leave the factory early. But a second knock sounded at his door.

"Come," Hugh repeated.

Mr. Bertrup poked his head inside again. "Sorry to disturb you once more, sir, but Maud Henley is here to see you."

Why had Ned's mother come to see him? And did he have the strength for such a visit when the unspoken weight of Harry's death pressed heavily on his shoulders? Hugh considered putting off the meeting until tomorrow, yet he felt he owed it to Ned to find out what Maud wanted.

"I will see her."

Maud Henley stepped into his office and waited for his secretary to close the door before she spoke. "Do you have a moment, Mr. Whittington?"

"Yes, of course." She looked near to collapsing, which prompted his question, "Did you walk the entire way here?"

He was relieved when she shook her head. "I rode in Farmer Terry's cart for part of the way."

"Please," he said, coming around the desk and pulling out a chair for her. "Won't you have a seat?"

Hesitating only a moment, she sat, her hands curled

tightly around the handle of her purse. "I reasoned you'd wish to know..."

"Know?" The note of shock and resignation in her tone set Hugh immediately on edge.

Mrs. Henley lowered her chin and directed her next words toward her lap. "I learned from Ada yesterday that... that Ned has been killed."

"No." Hugh dropped onto the edge of his desk, a fresh wave of sorrow rocking through him. First Harry, and now Ned. "I'm so very sorry, Mrs. Henley."

When she glanced up, her eyes were filled with tears. "He was my only child." Her voice hitched with emotion. "Even when I heard he was leaving for France, I didn't believe he'd go before me."

"What mother does?" Certainly, Helena Whittington wasn't expecting such an outcome. "I am truly sorry for your loss, ma'am. Your son was one of the best of men I've ever had the pleasure of knowing." He coughed as his own grief threatened to engulf him. "I'm afraid I received word regarding Harry as well."

Her damp eyes widened, and she shook her head. "He's been...?"

"Yes." The affirmative answer tasted bitter against Hugh's tongue.

In the next moment, the woman was on her feet. "If I may, I wish to see your mother."

"She doesn't yet know. The telegram was delivered only a few minutes ago." Hugh stood as well. "I was on my way to Whitmore House to tell her the news. But if you wish to come along..."

Her nod was decisive. "I would, thank you. We grieving mothers must band together."

After telephoning his driver, Hugh led Mrs. Henley

outside to wait for the automobile. Neither of them spoke, though no words were necessary. They shared a bond of silent grief.

Did Ada have someone to share her grief with? he wondered later as the car rattled along the road. Hugh hoped so. The memory of his promise to Ned—to look after his wife and daughter—returned to his mind. He'd begin by writing Ada a letter of condolence, and he would pray for her, too. Then perhaps in time, he'd know if there was more he could do to keep his promise.

Ada dragged herself home from the warehouse, barely aware of getting there until she stood before Minnie's door. Thankfully, her work was rather mindless, or she probably would have been let go two weeks ago for being so distracted. She couldn't shake the cloud of grief and darkness that had shrouded her since receiving the news that Ned had been killed. She felt half-dead herself, moving woodenly through each day, even as she did her best to put on a cheerful face for Rosemary.

Squeezing her eyes shut, she reviewed in her mind the list of things she still needed to do before sleep—supper, dishes, bedtime story, and putting Rosemary to bed. Then Ada opened her eyes and knocked on the door. Her daughter and the O'Reilly children greeted her, their voices rising above each other's in happy chatter. She tried to pay attention, but her head ached.

"Sounds as if all of you had a marvelous day," she interjected.

Minnie appeared in the hallway. She took one look at

Ada and bustled the children back inside. "You and your mum can have supper with us tonight, Rosemary." Ada's daughter cheered at the news, along with the other children.

"Thank you, Minnie, but that really isn't—"

But her friend was already steering Ada out the door, calling back to the children, "Janey, you're in charge. I'll be back soon."

Minnie didn't stop shuffling her along until they reached the door to Ada's flat. Even then, she pried the key from Ada's hand and unlocked the door.

"Sit," she directed, guiding Ada to a kitchen chair before taking one for herself. "You 'ave to talk, Ada."

Removing her hat, she tossed it on the table. "I'm fine, Minnie. Just tired."

"Ha." Minnie shook her head, her green eyes throwing out sparks of indignation. "Don't think I can't tell what you're about. I've known you six years."

Ada peeled off her gloves. "What do you mean?" she asked, not bothering to hide her annoyance.

"You're not grievin' this time, Ada." Minnie leaned forward. "Not out loud at least."

The flicker of irritation grew. "I don't have time to grieve. I have a job and a daughter to raise on my own." Her voice trembled, which only added to her frustration. "But I'll manage."

"Suit yourself." Minnie stood. "Though I didn't take you for a coward."

Ada's mouth dropped open in shock. "A coward?" she repeated. "I lost my husband, Minnie." The words flew from her lips like bullets. "What is it about that which makes me a coward?"

"The loss don't," her friend said, her voice softer. "But 'iding all them feelings inside sure does."

Rising to her feet, Ada paced to the window, her arms folded tightly. She felt overwhelmed, as much by Minnie's accusations as by the emotions roaring to life inside her. But it hurt too much to feel. She wanted to return to the numbness, yet the thoughts she'd kept trapped for days now spilled from her mouth unbidden.

"You care to hear how I feel?" She didn't wait for Minnie's reply. "I will tell you. I feel so angry, I want to scream. I'm angry at God and at Ned and at this ridiculous war." Tears burned in her eyes as she went on, her volume rising. "I feel so gutted with grief, I sometimes wonder if I might die, too." She flinched at saying such a thing out loud, but Minnie didn't counter the remark with judgment.

"What else?" she gently prodded instead.

Ada gave a bitter laugh. "What, indeed? I detest climbing out of bed every morning, knowing I must face another day alone. I detest feeling weak in my faith, but maybe it will never be strong. I detest that half my heart feels as if it has stopped beating." The tears slipped down her cheeks. "Most of all, I detest that he's gone," she admitted as she turned, her voice hardly more than a whisper. "He's gone, Minnie. And he won't be returning."

"I know, love. I know." Minnie embraced her. "That's what you needed to get out."

When she could finally speak again, Ada asked the question foremost on her mind, "Am I horrible . . . for saying such things?"

"No, Ada. You're a grievin' widow." Her friend stepped back, though she kept hold of Ada's shoulders. "And a brave woman."

Ada smirked. "You claimed a moment ago that I was a coward."

"Ah, but that's just me way. I didn't mean a thing by it,

exceptin' to get you to talk." Minnie gave her a teasing smile. "I believe you're braver than you know."

With a sigh, Ada returned to her seat. Minnie did the same. "I don't feel brave. I keep praying for peace and courage, but I can't help wondering if anyone is even listening."

"'E is."

"How can you be sure?" she countered, hurt and yearning giving her tone a slight edge.

Minnie's look held understanding. "Because 'E made us friends, knowing we'd need each other as we 'ave. 'E hears and loves us, 'specially in the dark times when we wonder if'n anyone is there."

As she considered Minnie's confident assurances, something loosened inside Ada. The hardness fractured and slipped away from her heart—leaving it still sore with grief, but open and pliant, too.

"I find God often 'elps us through others," Minnie said. "'E also turns our ashes into beauty."

"Ashes into beauty?" Ada had never heard that before.

Minnie nodded. "It's one of my favorite scriptures. Isaiah 61:3." She climbed to her feet. "I'm goin' to finish supper now. Come when you're ready."

"Thank you." Ada rose from her chair. "Rosie and I are lucky to have you and Thomas and the children."

Tears glittered in her friend's eyes now. "We're the lucky ones. And don't you go forgettin' it. 'Specially the next time you go disappearin' into yourself."

"I won't." She offered Minnie a smile—and this time, it was not forced.

When her friend left, Ada went to the parlor. She took Ned's Bible from the shelf. Dust had collected along its top and spine. She wiped it away with her hand, then sat in the armchair. After a few moments, she located the verse that was Minnie's favorite.

"'To give unto them beauty for ashes,'" she read aloud, "'the oil of joy for mourning, the garment of praise for the spirit of heaviness; that they might be called trees of righteousness, the planting of the Lord, that He might be glorified.'"

A seedling of warmth and peace sprang inside her as she pondered the words—*beauty for ashes, joy for mourning, praise for heaviness.* Had her prayers been heard after all, though not in the way she had expected? Minnie's help today, however unconventional, and this feeling of comfort—were they possible evidences that God did hear and care about her?

Ada shut the Bible and stood, suddenly eager to be with her daughter and friends again. But as she moved toward the bookshelf to replace the volume in its slot, she had another thought. Carrying the Bible into her room, she set it on top of the bureau. It was well past time to start reading it for herself and finding her own favorite passages.

Several nights later, after Rosemary was in bed, Ada remembered the letter she'd received from Hugh Whittington more than a week ago but hadn't yet read. She'd guessed his reason for writing and hadn't wanted to read his condolences, however sincere. But now she felt able to do so. She sat on the sofa, grateful enough light filtered through the window to see by so there was no temptation to violate the lighting restrictions.

Hugh's letter began with deep sympathies for Ned's death, which Ada suspected he'd learned of from her mother-in-law. He also shared how much he'd respected Ned. Then he shared the news that his younger brother Harry had also been killed in action.

"Oh, Hugh," Ada whispered with a shake of her head. "Your poor mother."

Sorrow settled over her as she recalled what she could remember of the happy-go-lucky Harry. Ada wondered if he'd left behind a sweetheart in Yorkshire. A feeling of empathy welled up inside her. This war had produced so many grieving sweethearts, mothers, wives, sisters, brothers, and children. How many more would be added to their number before the conflict was over?

She returned her attention to Hugh's letter and was pleased to read that Maud and Mrs. Whittington had apparently become good friends through the shared grief of losing their sons. It was comforting to know that someone was there to console Maud in Ada's absence.

Hugh finished his missive with an offer to help in any way she might need. Emotion, namely gratitude, filled Ada's throat. She wouldn't soon forget Hugh's kindness in helping Ned find a position at the printer's as well as their flat, or his thoughtfulness in writing to her.

After locating her stationery, she began to pen a reply. She thanked Hugh for the letter and expressed her grief at hearing the news of his brother.

What else should I write? she wondered, tapping the pen against her chin.

It felt strange to write a letter to someone who wasn't Maud or her grandmother, especially a man. But soon enough, she was scribbling away, asking Hugh questions about the boot factory and sharing about her own work at the paper warehouse. After thanking him once more for writing, she signed her name.

On sudden impulse, Ada added a postscript. *As far as your request to be of help,* she wrote, *there's nothing we need at present. However, another letter would not be unwelcome.*

Should she scratch out that last sentence? It felt rather vulnerable to ask Hugh to write her again. But before she could change her mind, she sealed the missive in an envelope to post the following day.

She'd realized the importance of good friends this week, particularly in difficult times. And difficult times were what they all faced these days. Besides, the idea of exchanging a few more letters with an old family friend filled her with a glimmer of anticipation—and that was something she hadn't felt in a long time.

CHAPTER 12

Yorkshire, December 1916

HUGH SAT IN his study, his chair facing the window. A few snowflakes had fallen earlier, but it wasn't cold enough for the snow to linger on the ground for long. He was reading Ada's most recent letter. A story she told about eating fish, fish, and more fish had him chuckling.

Ada had always possessed a clever sense of humor, which meant her letters over the past four months had brought him immense delight and entertainment. She wrote frankly but comically about life in wartime London, including her experiences with night air raids, ration cards, and light restrictions. And while the war had certainly affected Yorkshire, Ada's experiences in the city were different from his own in the countryside.

In truth, he'd been rather surprised when Ada had written him back that first time, and more so when she'd asked if he would write her again. Hugh had promptly done so, and they'd been corresponding regularly since.

I believe I shall change professions, Ada wrote. *Become a special constable instead. Can't you see me strutting about the city in a dark uniform and peaked cap?*

Hugh laughed out loud at the image. A moment later, he heard someone at the study door. Turning, he found his mother standing there, eyeing him with blatant curiosity.

"What has you so amused?" Helena Whittington entered the room. "I have not heard you laugh like that in ages."

It was true. He hadn't laughed with such abandon in a long time. There were days when he still keenly missed his brother, but Ada's letters and his faith had been great comforts through the grief.

"It's a letter," he answered, folding it and placing it back into its envelope. "From Ada Henley."

"Ada Henley? She wrote to you?" Helena raised her eyebrows in surprise as she stepped toward him.

Standing, Hugh glanced down at his desk. "I wrote her first a few months ago, and we've exchanged some letters in that time."

"Does Maud know?" his mother asked. "Heavens, do her parents know?"

He lifted his chin. "Mamma, there is nothing wrong or untoward about writing Ada. We have been friends with her and the Thornes for years, and she is now a widow. Besides, her husband requested that I look after her and their daughter if something were to happen to him, and Ada expressly asked if I would be willing to correspond."

Helena appeared unaffected by his logical explanation, so Hugh added in a quiet voice, "She needs a friend."

"Very well." The look she gave him alerted him to the nature of her next words before she'd even voiced them. "I only wonder if that has been hard for you."

Hugh slipped his hands into his pockets and turned toward the window again. "My . . . feelings for her . . . are in the past. They have been ever since Henley told me they were planning to marry. Nothing on that score has changed."

"I'm relieved to hear it," Helena said, her voice full of motherly compassion. "I don't wish to see you hurt, Hugh."

Facing her again, he offered what he hoped was a convincing smile. "She did not hurt me, because she never knew what I felt for her. And that is how it will stay."

"Splendid." She moved toward the door, where she paused. "It is nice to hear you laughing again. As you used to . . . with Harry." He caught the sheen of tears in her eyes. "If, as your friend, Ada inspires such laughter, I shall be grateful for it."

"Thank you."

She smiled fully at him. "Perhaps she and her little girl wouldn't mind a few gifts for Christmas. That would be another way to help." Her eyebrows rose with hinted amusement before she exited the room.

Christmas gifts? Hugh wished he'd thought of that sooner, though there might still be time to send something. Twisting his chair around, he sat back down, pulled out a fresh sheet of paper, and began to make a list.

Seated in the armchair, her robe wrapped snugly around her, Ada tucked her stocking feet beneath her nightgown. Wisps of white snow fell beyond the window on this Christmas morning. Rosemary sat on the rug, admiring the doll that had been a gift to her from Ada's grandmother.

It wasn't the only present they'd received, either. Maud had sent a pretty card, and Hugh had surprised Ada with a whole crate of gifts, including a ham. She had no idea how he'd managed to procure the meat, but she was deeply grateful to have something other than fish to eat today. She wished that she'd thought to send him something, too, in addition to the Christmas postcard she'd mailed along with her latest letter. Their renewed friendship had come to mean a great deal to her.

The sight of Rosemary happily playing with her doll's matching dark hair and intricate clothes stirred both pleasure and pain in Ada. She relished these carefree moments with her daughter, yet on this joyous holiday, she also ached with missing Ned.

"She is quite a beautiful doll, Rosie."

Rosemary lifted her head and beamed. "Yes, she is, Mummy."

"We must write and thank Gran. And Mr. Whittington as well." She'd explained earlier that Hugh was an old friend of her and Ned's.

"I can write the words all by myself now that I'm in school." Her blue eyes—Ned's eyes—shone with pride.

Ada smiled. "You certainly can. Now, come sit with me, pet. I have a present for you, too."

"What is it?" her daughter asked, jumping up from the rug.

Drawing Rosemary onto her lap, Ada reached into the pocket of her robe and removed the tiny locket she'd purchased. Her daughter and Janey loved to play with Ada's glass jewelry, but this was something Rosemary could wear now.

"Happy Christmas, Rosie." She handed her the locket.

Rosemary held it as if it were fashioned with diamonds. "A real necklace? For me?"

"Indeed." A laugh bubbled out of Ada at her daughter's raptured expression, and she playfully tapped her on the nose. "Take a look inside."

Her daughter's small fingers took a moment to work the

even smaller clasp, but finally she had it open. Inside the locket, Ada had placed a picture of herself on one side of the tiny oval and a picture of Ned on the other.

"It's me and Daddy." She wrapped her arms around Rosemary.

At first, she'd been reluctant to cut up the photograph of their family they'd taken during Ned's leave, but Ada's desire to help her daughter remember her father had outweighed her hesitation. Besides, she still had Ned's copy of the photograph, which had arrived with the rest of his personal effects some weeks after the telegram announcing his death.

"Wherever you go, when you wear your necklace, Daddy and I will be with you."

Rosemary rested her head against Ada's chest. "Even at school?"

"Even at school."

"I've a present for you, too, Mummy." She hopped off Ada's lap and ran into the bedroom. A few moments later, she raced back into the parlor with a scrap of paper in her hand. "I wrote it myself."

Ada took the paper. It appeared to have been painstakingly made into a pocket of sorts. On the outside, her daughter had written the words *To Mummy, Love Rosemary*. A peek inside revealed a single lock of Rosemary's hair.

"Minnie cut it. From right here." Rosemary indicated a shorter strand near her face as she leaned against Ada's knee. "I didn't use the scissors, honest. Do you like it?" Her gaze met Ada's, full of childlike expectation.

"I adore it, Rosie." She pulled her daughter onto her knees once more and kissed her forehead.

"If you keep it in your pocket," Rosemary said, twisting a button on Ada's nightgown, "then I'll always be with you, too. Even when you go to the warehouse."

"Then that is what I shall do."

Holding her daughter close, Ada shut her eyes and let the tears slip out. Tears of joy for this sweet little girl and the kindness of others, and tears of heartache at Ned's absence.

"Why are you crying, Mummy?" Rosemary's fingers brushed at Ada's cheeks.

She sniffed and opened her eyes. "Sometimes, we cry when we are happy, pet. And sometimes, we cry when we are sad."

Rosemary studied her. "Which one are you?"

"Today, I feel a bit of both," she said, fingering one of her daughter's curls.

"Happy because it's Christmas, but sad because Daddy's gone."

"Yes, Rosie. You are exactly right."

Her daughter gave her a smile, though it soon drooped. "I miss Daddy, too. Is he off fighting like William's daddy?"

More tears dropped onto Ada's nightgown as she shook her head. Rosemary had asked this question before, and each time, Ada cringed before answering. But she wouldn't lie to her daughter. "No, pet. Remember, your daddy is in Heaven now."

"Then he's safe," Rosemary declared with wisdom well beyond her five years.

Ada hugged her again. "Yes, Rosie, he is safe and watching over us. Just as God is."

"Is it fine if that makes me happy?"

She rested her cheek on her daughter's hair. "It's quite fine. I feel happy knowing that, too."

After a few moments, Ada set Rosemary on her feet. "Shall we get dressed? Then we can take Gran's gifts over to William and his family."

"Oh, yes." Rosemary grinned. "Can I wear my necklace?"

"Of course."

The doll in one hand, the locket in the other, she skipped into the bedroom to change. Ada stood, clasping Rosemary's gift to her chest.

Her gaze went to the mantel, where she'd placed their family photograph beside the clock. "Happy Christmas, Ned," she whispered. "I believe it might be a happy one after all."

Chapter 13

June 1917

ADA HAD BARELY finished eating her dinner when a distant *boom* rattled the windows of the paper warehouse. Instinctively, she dropped to the floor. It couldn't be the German zeppelins. They only dropped their deadly presents at night.

"Whatever might that be?" Lillie asked from where she'd crouched beside Ada. The rest of their coworkers were hunched down as well, regarding each other with puzzled or frightened expressions.

Ada shook her head. "Hopefully not a factory explosion."

The booming repeated itself again, then again. Ada flinched each time. The noise sounded too much like bombs to her liking. Whatever the source, the consequences weren't likely to be good.

A worm of fear slithered through her at not knowing what was going on or who was being affected. Was Rosemary all right? Ada had always been with her during the night air raids. But she couldn't be with her daughter now, to offer comfort.

That left only one thing to do—pray.

Ada prayed Rosemary would be safe, along with Minnie and her children. Janey and William were both ill, so they hadn't joined Rosemary at school today.

Surely, they would all be fine, she tried to reassure herself. If these were airships dropping bombs on London, they would be targeting warehouses and factories, not schools or civilian housing. If anything, she and her fellow workers were in greater danger than her daughter and their friends. And, if something should happen to her, Ada took solace from the knowledge the O'Reillys would step in to care for Rosemary.

Her mother-in-law would have been the first to do so, but Maud had passed away in the spring. Ada had wanted to attend the funeral—Hugh had offered to pay the train fare for her and Rosemary—but she couldn't take time away from the warehouse and still hope to have employment when she returned. So she'd stayed in London, her heart aching for weeks afterward at not being able to formally honor Maud.

When silence finally descended once more over the warehouse, the supervisor ordered everyone back to work. Ada climbed to her feet and followed Lillie and Belinda to one of the mounds of paper. A strained quiet filled the warehouse as they returned to their tasks.

Sometime later, Lillie nudged Ada before motioning to the door. "S'pose she's lookin' for a job?"

Ada glanced at the warehouse entrance to find Minnie standing there. "That is my friend and neighbor," she said with surprise.

What was Minnie doing here? Ada lifted her hand in greeting, but Minnie didn't return the gesture. Instead, she turned her back to the room. Something was definitely amiss.

After making certain the supervisor wasn't nearby, Ada hurried over to her friend. "What is it? Are the children worse?"

Minnie turned, but at the sight of her white face and haunted gaze, Ada stepped back in alarm. "Is it Thomas?" she asked in a whisper. *Don't let it be another telegram, Lord. Please.*

"It's not Thomas, but ..." Minnie pressed her lips together and began wringing her hands.

The dread inside Ada grew, clawing at her throat. Glancing back at her fellow workers, she steered Minnie outside. "Whatever is the matter, Minnie?"

"I only just 'eard." Her voice hitched as she stared at the ground. "There's been a terrible accident..."

"An accident? Where?"

Minnie lifted her chin, her gaze tortured. "At the school, Ada." She seemed to force the next words from her mouth. "A ... a bomb 'it the building. More than a dozen children were ... were killed. They're still pullin' out the survivors."

The breath left Ada's lungs, and her knees sagged. Minnie quickly reached out a hand to support her. "Wh-what about Rosie?" She fingered her daughter's lock of hair that she always kept inside her pocket. Rosemary was fine—she had to be.

Tears slid down Minnie's cheeks. "I knew you'd want to know, so I left the children at 'ome and went to see. I tried to slip past the constable, but 'e weren't letting anyone near. I tried, Ada, I did."

"Is my daughter hurt?" She didn't care that she now sounded hysterical. "She's not hurt, is she?"

Her friend's expression of empathy and hesitation was nearly too painful to see. "I-I don't know."

"I'm going to see." She squared her shoulders and started marching in the direction of the school. If she lost her position for walking out without permission, so be it. She would break in two if she didn't learn the fate of her daughter this instant.

"I'll come with." Minnie fell into step beside her.

Though she didn't say it, Ada was grateful for the company.

She kept putting one foot in front of the other, surrounded by a cloud of shock that muted the sights and sounds around them. As Minnie had explained, they were stopped well before they reached the school. But Ada would not be deterred. She demanded the constable allow them to pass. "Our children attend that school," she told him. "Please, let us by."

The man fiddled with the brim of his cap, his long mustache twitching, then he gave them a look of pity and waved them forward. Instinctively, Ada thanked him—the product of a lifetime of politeness and good breeding, something so ingrained, it functioned without conscious thought, even in the midst of such mind-numbing uncertainty.

The sound of sobbing hit her like a tidal wave before the actual destruction and chaos came into view. Children, teachers, and families huddled together some distance from the school. Except the familiar, solid building Ada had seen that morning was now a mound of rubble and brick. The horrifying sight made her pause, but just for a moment.

"Rosemary Henley?" she said to the first woman she saw. "Have you seen Rosemary Henley?"

The woman shook her head, her expression one of distress and empathy. Panic burned cold inside Ada as she and Minnie moved on, both of them questioning everyone they came across. She had to find her daughter.

"Mrs. Henley?" One of the teachers approached. The woman's face was streaked with grime, her dress dirty and tattered. But it was the dazed look in her red eyes that speared Ada to the core. "I'm so very sorry, ma'am." The words, though surely meant to be sincere, sounded a bit rote. How many times had those at the school been forced to say them today?

The teacher held something in her fist. It caught the weak sunlight as she opened her fingers to reveal the object. "This was found amongst the rubble."

It was Rosemary's locket.

Ada felt suddenly detached from everything and everyone. Surely, this couldn't mean that her daughter ... Minnie latched on to her arm, and she felt a flicker of gratitude at having something solid to lean on. As if in a dream, she watched herself extend her hand toward the woman and take hold of the locket. She crushed the chain against her palm, desperate to feel something.

"The bomb fell right through the roof." The teacher visibly swallowed. "Through the boys' class and the girls'. And then exploded in the infant class."

Rosemary's class.

Ada closed her eyes, wishing she could unhear those awful words. Wishing she was back in the flat with Rosemary ... and Ned. Oh, how she longed to have him here with her now.

"What do I—"

Her question was cut off by a high-pitched cry. "I want my mummy! Where's my mummy?"

The child's voice should have been lost among the wailing, the shouts, and the confusion, but somehow, Ada heard it. "Rosie?" she whispered, glancing toward a nearby group of students and mothers. Had she imagined her little girl's cry?

"I have to find my mummy!"

There was no mistaking her daughter's shout this time. "Rosie!" Ada cried as she rushed forward, her heart beating so hard with hope that it hurt. The crowd parted, and there was her daughter, seated on the ground.

"Oh, pet." Ada sunk to her knees beside Rosemary and gathered her close in a tight embrace. Never, ever would she let go. "Rosie, I'm here," she soothed through her own tears. "Mummy's here."

Her daughter squirmed within her grip. "My head hurts."

Ada released her to arm's length, just far enough to see the ugly, bloodied gash on the girl's forehead. In that moment, the fog of shock inside her head disappeared. "We need to get you to the hospital right away."

Scooping her daughter into her arms, Ada turned to Minnie. "Do you mind returning to the warehouse and telling them what has happened?"

"Not to worry," Minnie said, nodding. She pressed a quick kiss to Rosemary's cheek. "You and William both need to get well now, you 'ear?" The declaration prompted a tiny smile from Rosemary, as Ada suspected her friend had intended.

She freed one hand to take hold of Minnie's and gave it a squeeze. "Thank you." Minnie had not only accompanied her on her dreadful errand, but she knew her friend had felt all the fear, panic, and relief as keenly as Ada had. "Hopefully, we will be home by evening."

As Minnie walked away, Ada carried Rosemary toward a waiting ambulance. "We will have you stitched up in no time, pet."

"Will it hurt?"

Ada wanted to weep at the simple question, especially in light of all that her daughter and the others at the school had experienced today. Including those whose children hadn't survived. She tightened her hold around Rosemary. "It may hurt, and I promise to be right there beside you."

"Just like God?"

Fresh tears leaked from Ada's eyes as she nodded. "Just like God."

"Was He with us when I heard that horrible noise and hit my head?"

"Yes," Ada managed to say over the lump in her throat. "He was with each and every one of you, and He understands your fear and pain."

Just as He did mine when Ned died.

It had been nearly a year, and Ada had been growing her faith ever since by reading from the Bible each night and taking Rosemary to church with the O'Reillys on Sundays. But it wasn't until this moment that she was able to view that awful day last summer with more clarity than she ever had.

With perfect empathy, her Father in Heaven had understood the intensity of her pain over losing her husband. He also understood the intense relief she'd felt at finding her daughter alive today. And, Ada suddenly realized, He wasn't any less present or loving in one experience than the other—He'd been with her during both.

She recalled something Ned had told her before leaving to be a soldier—about how God knew what a person needed to grow, even if that growth meant experiencing pain. The Lord was present in her pleasant experiences as well as her painful ones, and He was willing to help her learn and grow through that pain.

Giving beauty for ashes, she reminded herself as the deep hope she'd been yearning to feel for so long filled her heart to overflowing.

Chapter 14

"I must go to London at once." Hugh threw down his napkin and stood up from the breakfast table.

Helena frowned. "Whatever for?"

"It's in regards to Ada." He lifted the letter in his hand. "Or rather, her daughter, Rosemary. Or the both of them, maybe. I'm not yet sure."

"Will you please sit down and kindly explain yourself?"

He ignored the invitation to take his seat again. "The other day, German bombers hit London, and one of the bombs they dropped struck Rosemary's school." His mother gasped, eliciting another cringe of horror from him as well. Ada had left off the raw details, but she'd shared enough to give him a fair idea of what a horrific scene it had been.

"Was the little girl . . ."

Hugh shook his head. "No. Other than a cut on her head, she is fine."

"Oh, thank goodness." His mother's hand had risen to rest against her heart, making Hugh wonder if she was feeling again some of the pain of losing her own child to this war. "I'm sincerely relieved to hear they are unhurt. However, if that is the case, then why must you go to London at all?"

"Because . . ." He frowned, exasperated by the return of her calm demeanor. "Her daughter was nearly killed, Mamma. She lost her husband last year, and her mother-in-law this spring."

Helena shot him an arched look, but he couldn't tell if it was in response to his outburst or his obvious deep concern for Ada.

Relaxing his chokehold on the letter, he fought to speak evenly. "I believe Ada needs my help."

"Has she asked for such a thing?"

He thought back through what he'd read. "Well, no, but—"

"Hugh, there is something I must share with you." She paused, and he realized she wasn't going to say anything more until he sat. Fighting a growl, he pulled back his chair and resumed his seat. Helena smiled in approval. "It's something I clearly failed to teach you after your father died."

This was a turn in the conversation he hadn't expected. "And what is that?"

"You, my dear boy, are not responsible for the rest of us."

It took all of his willpower not to roll his eyes at the absurd statement. Of course he was responsible for the rest of them. Wasn't that the charge he'd been given by his father on the man's deathbed? "I don't wish to contradict you."

"Then don't," she said with a spark in her brown eyes as she bent forward. "What I'm saying is the truth. You may offer to help or speak words of comfort . . ." She waved a hand at his letter. "But you must stop trying to care for everyone, especially when they have not asked for it."

Her words stung, making him wish to dismiss them, which surely attested to the truth within them. "I'm sorry if I have overstepped my position as the eldest."

"Pish posh." She swatted away his apology as she sat back.

"This is not about position. This is about you learning to allow others to do and grieve and be as they see fit, darling." Her gaze turned wistful. "I am aware that is not what your father requested of you."

Hugh raised his eyebrows in disbelief. "Are you?"

"Yes," she said, nodding. "Your father meant well, but the burden he placed upon you was hardly fair. I'm not just talking about his encouraging your innate sense of responsibility for us, either."

He rubbed a hand over his jaw, feeling suddenly tired. "You are speaking of the factory?"

"The estate, too." His mother gave him a look that held only love and concern. "I realize now that your father should have asked you if you wished to oversee all of this."

"If I had said no, what then?" He couldn't believe he dared voice such a question, but a part of him wished he'd done so years ago.

Helena smiled. "We would have survived, though I don't believe the estate or the factory would have been as successful without you." She twisted her teacup in its saucer. "Is this still what you would choose?"

He blew out a breath as he considered it. A long-ago conversation with Ned Henley returned to his mind. Ned had asked him what he would do if he wasn't managing the estate and the boot factory. He didn't have an answer that day. But did he have one now?

Truth be told, there were days he rather liked overseeing the boot factory, and the estate was as dear to him as the people who had and did still occupy it. He'd found contentment in this life and had chosen contentment in it.

"I do still choose this." The assurance and confidence in his tone matched that inside his heart.

Helena's eyes brightened. "I'm glad to hear it. Now, about the other matter . . ."

"Of not taking responsibility?" Even saying the words out loud made him flinch. Duty and responsibility were as ingrained in him as boot making.

She gave a light laugh as if she could read his thoughts. Hugh didn't doubt there were times she could. "I'm not asking you to cease being responsible. That is an honorable trait in anyone. I'm asking you to allow others to develop that trait for themselves by not swooping in to help at any given moment. We learn best when we experience pain, my boy, or when we have to flounder a bit. Because of God's great love for us, He does not prevent discomfort or consequences. We must to do the same with others."

Hugh fingered the letter, his mind awhirl. "Then I suppose," he said at length, "I shall not be heading to London. At least not at present. I will ask Ada, again, if there is anything I might do for her. In the meantime, I suppose I will wait and pray."

"That, my darling, is the mark of a truly extraordinary, responsible man."

The compliment filled him with warmth and gratitude and made him wonder if he'd misjudged his mother's higher regard for Harry. Perhaps their bond had come because, unlike Hugh, his younger brother had often been more concerned with seeing and being with people rather than assuming responsibility for them. He felt a pang of regret at the realization.

"I'm sorry, Mamma." He glanced down at his half-eaten meal. "I have been so busy trying to prove myself and to care for everyone that I haven't taken as much time to understand or to simply sit and talk in this way."

She reached across the table and covered his hand with her own. "You do not have to prove yourself to anyone, my boy. You were needed here," she added with keen perceptiveness. "And my feeling is you still are, though I don't know all the reasons why."

Her words dropped into his heart and gently swept away his lingering remorse. "Thank you."

"You are most welcome." She pushed back her chair and stood. "I believe I will place more flowers on Maud's grave this morning."

Hugh sensed how much she missed her friend. While Helena still visited regularly with Ada's mother, she'd found a kindred spirit in Maud, despite their starkly different backgrounds. It was a friendship that would be difficult to replace.

"Why don't I join you?" he offered, rising to his feet as well. He could afford to be a bit late to the factory today, if it meant spending more time with his wise mother.

She looked momentarily surprised, then pleased. "I would like that very much."

Maidenhead, July 1917

From her spot on the picnic blanket, Ada watched Rosemary throwing stones into the meandering river. The three older O'Reilly children were doing the same, while Minnie attempted to keep two-year-old Molly from running headlong into the water. Their two-week holiday in Berkshire—courtesy of the generous donations to the convalescent fund for the families of the schoolchildren—was nearly at an end.

"Don't know that I'm wantin' to go back," Minnie murmured with a sigh, voicing Ada's own thoughts. "Neither do the children."

The calm and quiet of the countryside had been the perfect balm to all of their shattered spirits after the bombing. Rosemary still had nightmares about the awful event, but the bad dreams had been less frequent during their time away from London.

"I feel the same." Ada ran her hand across the blades of grass. She hadn't realized how much she'd missed the rural scenery until leaving the city behind for the first time in seven years. If only they could stay here forever. "I wonder how much one of those little cottages is to rent."

Minnie chuckled as she steered Molly back toward the blanket. "I don't 'ave a clue, but we'd be clambering over each other if we shared one like we've done 'ere."

A smile lifted Ada's mouth. They had been rather cramped at times with two women and five children in one cottage, but it had also been nice to have more people around. A wave of missing Ned washed through her. He would have enjoyed this holiday. It would have reminded him, as it did Ada, of Yorkshire and home.

Had she truly put Stonefield Hall and home in the same thought? Her smile drooped. Wasn't London still her home?

She didn't have an answer for her former question, but she did the latter. While she loved much about the city and the life she'd built there, since Ned's death, the flat had felt less like a home and more a place where she and Rosemary lived.

Thoughts of Stonefield morphed to ones about her parents. She couldn't help wondering how they were faring. Hugh never spoke of them in his letters. Her grandmother periodically did—apparently, Ada's father had been ill several times of late.

Ada hadn't written them since Rosemary had been a baby. Ceasing to do so had helped her grieve and make peace with everything, but it hadn't stopped the occasional longing for what could be. A large part of her still wished to see her mother and father again. They were, after all, her parents, and whether they acknowledged it or not, she was still their daughter. And she did wish to mend this rift.

If letters would not help, was there any other way to contact them? To know for herself if they'd softened their position after seven years?

Turning her attention to Rosemary again, she felt renewed relief that she hadn't lost her daughter in the recent tragedy. Her little girl was growing up, as Rosemary often professed, into a person of compassion, friendliness, and faith. Gratitude filled Ada. She and Ned had accomplished what they'd hoped for with their family.

If only her parents could see that. Could see how Ada had grown and changed while in London, see how she was raising her daughter. While their values may differ from hers, she wanted to give Rosemary a full life—and that included one with extended family relationships as well as dear friends.

A sudden idea had her sitting up straight and made her pulse race with equal parts anticipation and anxiety. What if she took Rosemary to live in Yorkshire? There was little left for them in London, except for memories and reminders of loss. They could live with her grandmother, and Ada could find a position somewhere nearby to support them. And maybe a personal visit to her parents would accomplish what her letters hadn't. Perhaps the three of them could finally reconcile.

"What's that look in your eye, Ada?" Minnie studied her shrewdly. "I know that determined glint."

She gave a light laugh. How many times through the years had Minnie been there to comfort, support, and cheer her? Far more than Ada could count. She would only go forward with this plan of hers if her dearest friend agreed to join her in the countryside.

"I would like to go to Yorkshire." When Minnie's eyes widened in surprise, Ada hurried to explain. "I wish for Rosemary to know my grandmother better. And truth be told, I'm hoping she can come to know my parents as well."

The expression on Minnie's face registered understanding, along with a touch of dismay. "It's a grand idea. 'Ow long would you be gone?"

Ada shook her head. "It wouldn't be for a visit. We would stay there."

"Ahh." Minnie frowned at the grass. "Suppose I knew this day 'ad to come eventually."

"No, Minnie." She rose to her knees, eager to explain her full plan. "I wish for you to come, too. You and your children."

"What?" Minnie hopped up and grabbed the runaway Molly once again. "We wouldn't be welcome in that big ol' fancy 'ouse of yours," she said, talking over Molly's protests. "Not me and mine."

Ada extracted Molly from her mother's arms and placed Rosemary's neglected doll into the girl's hands to entertain her. "I'm not sure I will be welcome at Stonefield. Which is why I need to see if Gran would be willing to allow our families to live with her for a bit."

"But 'ow would we get on? We can't rely on your gran's charity."

Lifting her hand, Ada smoothed back Molly's red hair. "We would likely have to seek employment. But imagine this. The children can attend school in the village and run free around the countryside, just as they have here. No more bombs or smelly streets or constant noise."

A wistful look settled onto her friend's face as Minnie looked at Janey, William, and Alroy, laughing and playing by the river. "That'd be downright 'eavenly. But you still 'aven't said what we'd do for work."

A line from her grandmother's most recent letter returned to Ada's mind. "Gran is actually looking for a new cook. And you, Minnie O'Reilly, are the best cook I know. She may even have work for Thomas to do when he returns. As for me, I'm sure I shall find something."

Minnie's reflective demeanor deepened. "You truly want to see your parents again? You've told me 'ow they don't value what you do."

"It won't be without difficulty," she admitted as some of her apprehension crept back in, "but I believe it's not impossible. Even then, I don't plan to give up what is important to me. I can still teach Rosemary about faith and love, regardless of where we live."

Minnie nodded encouragingly. "Don't I know it."

"Thank you." Her confidence eased some of Ada's trepidation. "So what do you say? Will you come to Yorkshire with us?"

She held her breath as she waited for Minnie's answer. Regardless, she knew this what she needed to do, though she hated the possibility of no longer living near her dearest friend.

"You sure your gran would take in me and my wee ones?"

Was Minnie considering it? Ada let her breath out in a rush. "She would, indeed," she reassured. "Does this mean you'll come?"

"Aye." Minnie smiled. "We'll come."

Smiling again, Ada hugged little Molly. "I'm so relieved, because I am determined not to have any more goodbyes in my life for a very long time."

Chapter 15

As she stared up at the ornately carved front door of Stonefield Hall, Ada drew in a deep breath and released it slowly. She clutched Rosemary's hand tightly inside her own. Minnie and her children were happily ensconced at Gran's home, where the seven of them had slept the night before. The past few days had been a whirlwind of activity—returning to London from Berkshire, packing up their trunks, and taking the train north.

Now it was time to face her parents.

"You used to live here, Mummy?" Rosemary's awed tone drew a brief smile from Ada.

She gently squeezed her daughter's hand. "I did. And this is where your grandmother and grandfather live." She'd been preparing Rosemary for this meeting, so her daughter could better manage things if Ada's parents refused to see them.

Has it really been seven years? she thought, with a shake of her head. The last time she'd stood in front of the Georgian-style, red-brick house, she'd been young and very much in love. Now she was twenty-five, a widow, and a mother.

"Should we knock?" Rosemary glanced up at her.

Ada chuckled. "I suppose we should." Squaring her

shoulders, she gave the door a self-assured knock, though inside, she felt far from confident.

An older man she didn't recognize opened the door. Where had their dutiful butler gone? Off to war, perhaps. The change in staff saddened Ada. Had her maid, Hetty, left, too? Life hadn't stayed the same at Stonefield, in spite of Ada's belief over the years that it had.

"I wish to speak with Mr. Thorne," she said politely.

The man shook his head. "I'm afraid the master is feeling poorly and is not receiving visitors today."

Ada frowned at the troubling news. Her grandmother hadn't mentioned that Charles Thorne had taken ill again. "I'm sorry to hear he is unwell. I am hoping that he might still be able to speak with his daughter." Was this as far as they would get? Or would the butler allow them entrance?

His bushy gray eyebrows shot upward as he eyed them with barely veiled curiosity. "I apologize, Miss Thorne," he said, stepping back and opening the door for them.

"It's Mrs. Henley." Relieved at gaining admittance into the house, she guided her daughter inside. "This is my daughter, Rosemary."

"Miss Rosemary." The butler nodded.

Ada was pleased to see that the furnishings and marbled floor of the spacious entryway were just as she remembered. "Is my father in the library?" She glanced toward the door on their left.

"No, Mrs. Henley. He's in his sitting room."

It was her turn for surprise. Before she'd left home, her father had rarely used his sitting room during the day. "May I go up?" Though it felt strange to ask, this was no longer her house.

"Of course," the butler said, giving her a bow.

"Thank you."

She and Rosemary moved toward the staircase. The polished banister felt familiar beneath Ada's gloved hand as she guided her daughter up the steps. The wall paneling and paintings, the window seat on the landing, all of it was etched in her memory. Yet, in many ways, she was a stranger here. She'd lived a good portion of her life outside these walls, and the time away had changed her. She was no longer the bright-eyed, untried young woman she'd been back then—a truth for which she was grateful, whatever her parents might think.

The upstairs carpet muffled their footsteps as she and Rosemary made their way down the hall. Outside the door to her father's sitting room, Ada stopped.

"You wait here, pet, while I go in," she said, crouching beside Rosemary. If her parents rejected her outright, she wished to spare her daughter as much of the unpleasantness as possible.

Rosemary dipped her chin in a solemn nod, her eyes wide as she continued to take in the lavish surroundings. Ada saw her situated on a tufted armchair in the hallway, then she turned to face the sitting room door.

Her heart tripped faster and faster, her palms clammy inside her gloves. She'd prayed again and again the past few days about her decision. Each time, she'd felt a sense of rightness about moving to Yorkshire. However, she also recognized that didn't mean things with her parents would go splendidly today.

Exhaling slowly, she turned the handle, pushed open the door, and entered the room. Her mother was bent over her embroidery, her chair drawn up beside the sofa, where Ada's father sat.

Victoria Thorne glanced up first. When she saw Ada, she dropped her sewing to the floor and covered her mouth with both hands.

"Hello, Mamma." Ada crossed the room, keeping her back straight and her steps unrushed. Despite wearing a dress that was long past new and shoes that were well-worn, she would still conduct herself as a lady.

As she drew closer, Charles Thorne looked at her. Ada had to fight to keep her mouth from dropping open. His cheeks were sunken, and his dark eyes appeared overly large in his gaunt face. He seemed to have shriveled into himself since she'd last seen him. Clearly, whatever ailed him was not the temporary thing she'd thought. The realization stirred her compassion.

"Ada?" he said, his voice hoarse. The anguished plea in that one word was her undoing. She rushed forward, no longer hesitant or afraid, and dropped to her knees beside him.

"Yes, Papa, it's me." She clasped his hand in hers.

Victoria moved to kneel beside Ada, her cool fingers smoothing back Ada's hair, her eyes full of shock and happiness. "Whatever are you doing here, my dear? Has something happened?"

"Ned is gone," Ada stated in a matter-of-fact tone. The words hurt to voice aloud, yet the pain of losing her husband no longer cut as deeply or intensely as it once had. "He was killed last year in France."

A flicker of what might have been regret passed over the faces of her parents before it disappeared. But Ada had seen it, and it gave her hope.

"You have decided to come home, then?" her father asked, his tone wary.

She swallowed hard but nodded. "I would like to, yes."

"Of course, dearest." Her mother crushed her in a tight embrace. "We have wanted that for so long."

Would they have accepted her so willingly if she'd

brought Ned with her? She didn't know for certain, but she wouldn't waste time and energy questioning something that was no longer possible.

Victoria eased back and regarded Ada fully. "Look at you. You are more beautiful than when you left."

Words and stories rose to Ada's lips. She wished to tell them that any difference in her appearance had everything to do with the state of her heart and the peace she'd found in her faith. Yet she couldn't bear the thought of their skepticism if she tried to explain. So the moment passed.

As she studied her parents, her thoughts became crowded with painful memories. The returned letters, the tears, the decision to stop writing. How many times had she cried over their refusal to accept her husband and the life she'd created away from Stonefield Hall? And suddenly, she needed to know why.

"Why did you return my letters?" She addressed her father, maintaining a level gaze, even as his narrowed in defense.

A surprised gasp from her mother accompanied Ada's question. Had Victoria not known about the letters Ada had sent them, sent her? A glance at her mother's shocked, pale face confirmed her suspicions.

"I hoped to make amends, but you rejected every attempt. You pretended as if I had died." Her voice choked on the last word as recollections of nearly losing Rosemary flooded her mind. The years of frustration and pain at her parents' silence rose fresh inside her. "Why?"

Her parents exchanged a cryptic look, yet to Ada's surprise, it was her mother who answered. "We only wished for you what every parent desires for their child—that they grow up to be happy."

"I understand that, truly, I do." Especially as a parent

herself now. "The truth is I did find happiness, then and now. And while our definition of what makes us happy may differ, was that a reason to cut me off?"

Charles directed his words to a point above Ada's head. "We wished the best for you, Ada."

"Was staying silent the best for me?" She didn't bother to hide the hurt from her tone.

He ran a slightly trembling hand down his jaw. "Not exactly, no. But we ... I ... thought it might induce you to come home sooner."

"That is not why I'm here now."

"Why have you come home?" Victoria asked, glancing between her husband and daughter.

Ada straightened. "Because I know the importance of family."

"Then might you ..." Charles coughed, his dark eyes cloudy with what Ada understood was contrition. "Might you be willing to forgive us?"

She knew what it cost his pride to voice such a question. One she'd never heard from him while living here. "Yes, Papa." Her voice quavered with emotion. "I forgive you."

"Both of us?" Victoria was staring down at her hands as if she didn't recognize them now that they were bereft of her usual needle and thread.

Ada waited until her mother looked up again before she nodded. "Both of you," she whispered. In that moment of forgiveness, she felt the final splinter of her resentment shrink and disappear.

"Do you truly wish to make Stonefield your home once again?" Her father watched her with what appeared to be equal parts uncertainty and hope.

"Yes, I should like to live here."

Victoria hugged her a second time. "It will be as if you never left."

The careless declaration tore at Ada's fragile joy over their reunion. Things could not be as if she had never left, at least not for her. She'd found herself in London, and she would never wish for it to be otherwise or to return to the person she'd been.

Doubt riddled her resolve. It was one thing to forgive her parents; it was another entirely to return to this life of pageantry and wealth, where faith played so little a role. Could she submit to having servants wait on her when she was capable of doing those same tasks, and more, on her own? Could she continue to exemplify to her daughter the qualities she valued if they lived on the estate?

A desire to flee back to London, where things were familiar, rose inside Ada. Yet another glance at her father's wasting figure and her mother's jubilant expression made her pause in retracting her answer.

Just as she hadn't been alone in the city, she was not alone here. She had Minnie and her family nearby. God would be with her, too, as she continued to turn to Him for help and courage.

"There is one thing I should like to make clear," she said, rising, "if I am to come home for good."

Charles sat back and eyed her cautiously. "What is that?"

"I would ask that you accept my daughter as mine and Ned's, and allow me to raise her as I see fit." Ned was no longer with her, but Ada would always have pieces of him through Rosemary. She saw him in their daughter's bright blue eyes, in her kindness, and in her zest for life.

"Your daughter is with you?" Victoria asked in a delighted voice as she returned to her seat. "I may finally meet my grandchild."

"You knew about Rosemary?"

Victoria nodded, her smile soft. "Gran told me."

"Let us see the child," Charles said.

Ada didn't move. "Will you abide by my wishes?" Her loyalty remained with Rosemary. Even if that meant leaving her parents and Stonefield behind forever, she would do so to protect her daughter.

"Yes, Ada." His entire demeanor sagged. But perhaps it was as much from defeat as from relief that the rift between them had closed—at last.

Exiting the room, Ada held out her hand to Rosemary. Her daughter brightened at seeing her. She hopped off the chair and slipped her hand into Ada's. Together, they walked into the sitting room.

"Mamma, Papa, this is mine and Ned's daughter, Rosemary Henley."

Victoria beamed. "Come here, Rosemary."

Her daughter peered up at Ada. "You may go," she reassured her as she guided Rosemary closer.

"She looks so much as you did when you were a little girl," Victoria murmured. "How old are you, Rosemary?"

"Five."

Charles stared between Rosemary and Ada and back again as if he couldn't quite believe his little girl had a daughter of her own. "Do you care for sweets, Rosemary?"

The girl dipped her head in a nod.

"Ah, so did your mother." A brief smile softened his face as he leaned forward. "I believe Cook might have some sweets tucked away somewhere. What do you say we have them brought up?"

"Right now?" Rosemary's eyes widened.

He chuckled. "Right now." He pulled the bell cord to alert one of the servants, then patted the empty spot next to him on the sofa. "While we wait, you can tell us all about what other things you enjoy."

Once seated beside her father, Ada drew Rosemary onto her lap. She let her daughter answer her parents' questions, content to simply listen. The meeting she'd both anticipated and feared was over. In many ways, it had gone better than her expectations.

Still, she knew that did not mean the way forward would be easy or smooth. Her parents had accepted her and Rosemary and agreed to let Ada bring up her daughter as she wished. However, she knew they didn't fully understand yet how vastly different her choices and dreams were from theirs. She would not be adopting their way of life again, no matter how much they wished it or insisted.

Help me stay true to the lessons You've taught me while I've been away, Lord, she pleaded silently as she rested her chin on her daughter's curls. *Help us both find true happiness here.*

Hugh helped his mother out of the automobile, then looped her arm through his. Facing the old stone church, he pulled in a long breath, hoping to assuage the nerves eating at him. He was almost certain Ada would be in attendance at services today. What he was less certain about was how he felt at the prospect of seeing her in person for the first time in years.

The letter she'd sent him the other week had shocked him—Ada was coming home to Yorkshire and hoped to reconcile with her parents. And while Hugh was hopeful things between her and the Thornes would be resolved, he was saddened at the thought of no longer exchanging letters with her. He'd come to treasure those missives and the friendship that had grown between them through their correspondence.

How would things change now that she had returned? Would their interactions now consist of only seeing one another at church on Sundays and the occasional meal at Stonefield Hall or Whitmore House?

His mother shot him a questioning glance. She was likely curious as to why he was hesitating outside the building. Or perhaps she already knew the answer and was hoping to nudge him into action.

Whatever the reason for her look, he squared his shoulders and led her inside the church. Hugh didn't see Ada among those already seated. Disappointed, he sat beside his mother on the Whittington pew. Before long, the priest began the meeting. Hugh glanced over his shoulder, but he couldn't turn far enough around to see those behind him without calling undo attention to himself. Facing forward again, he did his best to concentrate on the service.

He rose with the rest of the congregation when the meeting concluded. His gaze went to the Thornes' pew midway toward the back. It hadn't been occupied by any member of the family for years, save for Christmas and Easter. But Ada wasn't sitting there.

Oh well, he told himself. She'd likely be in attendance next Sunday, or perhaps she'd visit Whitmore House...

Then he saw her, standing near the door of the church. A little girl, who Hugh guessed must be Rosemary, stood beside her. Ada was talking with several other members of the congregation.

He tried not to openly stare as he and his mother moved down the aisle toward them, but it was a difficult task. Ada was no longer the girl of eighteen she'd been when Hugh had last seen her. She'd always been lovely, yet now she radiated strength, beauty, and conviction.

Her dark-eyed gaze met his as she ended her other

conversation. Hugh's heart traitorously thumped faster when she smiled at him. He remembered that dazzling, almost impish smile of hers, but it was a new thing altogether to have it directed at him.

"Hugh Whittington," she said warmly. She stepped forward to greet him. "It has been ages, yet with all of our letters, I feel as if we saw each other just yesterday."

He nodded in agreement. "Welcome back."

"Thank you."

Helena reached out to clasp Ada's hand. "It is wonderful to see you again, my dear."

"A pleasure to see you, too, Mrs. Whittington."

"Are you and your daughter settling in?" Hugh guessed at what his mother was really asking—if Ada and her parents had come to an understanding.

"We are getting on well," Ada said to his great relief. "Mrs. Whittington, this is my daughter, Rosemary." She motioned to the girl at her side, then at Hugh. "Rosemary, this is Mr. Whittington. Remember he sent us those lovely gifts at Christmas?"

The girl offered them each a shy smile. "Hello."

"She looks so much like you, Ada." Helena bent forward to look Rosemary in the eye and smiled. "I knew your mother when she was your age."

"You did?"

"Do you know what she loved to do back then?"

Ada's daughter shook her head.

"Ride her horse." Helena straightened.

Rosemary turned wide blue eyes toward her mother. "You had a horse, Mummy?"

"I did," Ada said, laughing. The sound brought happy memories to Hugh's mind. "It's been far too long since I last rode, though."

He could easily recall what an excellent horsewoman she'd been. "I imagine you have not lost your skills, even after living in London."

"Perhaps I haven't."

Her daughter tugged on her hand. "Can I ride a horse, Mummy?"

"One of these days, pet." She returned her focus to Hugh and his mother. "My parents are hosting a party Saturday next to celebrate mine and Rosie's return." Her nose wrinkled in mild distaste, as if she found the idea of a party less enjoyable than she might have once. "You are both invited."

Hugh appreciated the invitation—and couldn't deny his anticipation at seeing her again soon—but he didn't fancy being one of many at the party, all vying for Ada's attention. He was already missing the easy camaraderie and privacy of their letters.

"We would love to come." Helena clutched his arm in a tight grip. "Wouldn't we, Hugh?"

"Yes," he answered.

Judging by her expression, Ada appeared relieved that they would be in attendance. That realization overrode his remaining reluctance.

"We shall expect you Saturday, then." She nodded to them before leading Rosemary out the door.

Hugh and his mother followed behind. When he didn't see the Thornes' vehicle waiting to take the pair home, he called after Ada, "Would you care to ride in our car?"

"Thank you, but no," she said, turning and giving him another charming smile. "We walked on purpose, so that I might take Rosemary to all of my favorite spots."

Had she shown her daughter the oak tree, Hugh wondered, where she and Ned used to meet? Other than the three of them, Hugh was certain no one else knew of the meeting place. He'd only known of it because he had happened to come across Ada standing there the first time she'd gone to meet Ned at the tree.

The memory tightened Hugh's chest, not with disappointment but with remembered pain. In that moment, he'd known Ada would never return his unspoken affection for her. It had taken a great deal of prayer and trust in God to be able to put his feelings to rest and support the courtship between her and his gamekeeper.

Would he have to face his regard for her once more now that Ada had returned a widow? Hugh almost feared the answer.

He tried to console himself with the knowledge that he'd buried those feelings once before—surely, he could do so again. More than his heart was at risk this time. His continued friendship with Ada was also at stake, and that friendship was something he would fight to keep in his life. Even if that meant fighting himself.

CHAPTER 16

ADA SLIPPED OUTSIDE and crossed the empty terrace. The summer air felt unusually cool against her flushed cheeks. Thankfully, it also chased from her nose the nauseating scents of perfume, cologne, and wealth that permeated her parents' guests. She felt a twinge of guilt at leaving a party that was meant to honor her return, but she needed a moment to herself.

The night had been a whirlwind of introductions, explanations, and conversations, all before the meal had been served. Rosemary had met most of the guests at the beginning of the party, then followed one of the maids upstairs to eat her supper. When the women had gone into the drawing room, Ada had excused herself to tuck her daughter into bed, listen to her nightly prayers, and read her a short story.

It felt strange to wear an evening gown again, one borrowed from her mother, and to listen to talk that didn't revolve around the costly price of eggs or which part of London had most recently been bombed. Ada had reluctantly returned to the party after Rosemary had fallen asleep. After the men had rejoined the ladies, her head had begun to ache.

She longed for a real discussion with someone like Hugh or his mother, but she'd been too bombarded by everyone else to exchange more than a few words with him and Helena.

If her father's health had been better, she would have protested having the party at all. But something inside whispered Charles Thorne might not be with them much longer, so Ada had agreed to go along with the event.

In the last week-and-a-half since she'd come home, the color had returned to her father's face, and he had been sitting up for longer periods of time. Unfortunately, according to his doctor, those weren't the signs of returning health.

"It's merely a rallying before the end," the man had confided two days earlier to Ada and Victoria. "I've witnessed such a thing in many of my patients."

Splaying her hands against the stone balcony, Ada glanced at the clouds overhead, wishing for a brief moment to be back in London. She missed having Minnie close by, though she and Rosemary walked to her grandmother's house nearly every day to see their friends.

She'd also navigated several heated discussions with her parents, who, in spite of their promise to allow Ada to raise her daughter as she wished, wanted to indulge Rosemary's every whim. But Ada was adamant that they not give her daughter material things as a way of securing her affection. It was a topic she feared they might never see eye to eye on, which meant more than one conversation with Rosemary about the value of friends and family—and how they were far more precious than any doll or sweet or cart pony, as wonderful as those things could be.

Hearing the sound of someone behind her, she turned to find Hugh approaching. The sight of him eased some of the tension in her head. "Mr. Whittington."

"Mrs. Henley."

She smiled as he came to stand beside her. "You are the first person, other than our butler, to address me correctly this evening."

"My sincerest apologies on behalf of your other guests."

A light laugh slipped from her lips. "Thank you, but I insist you call me Ada." After all, that's how he'd addressed her in his letters—letters she realized in this moment she missed receiving.

"Very well . . . Ada." He bowed slightly to her.

She liked hearing him say her name. "Thank you, Mr.—"

"No, no." He shook his head. "If I'm to call you Ada, then you must address me as Hugh."

Ada laughed again. "Good, because Mr. Whittington is much too formal."

"Agreed." He smiled warmly at her, reminding her of times long past when she'd been the beneficiary of this same pleasant, albeit somewhat infrequent, smile.

She'd once judged Hugh as being too serious. Yet after exchanging letters with him the past year, Ada knew differently. He was a gentleman in every respect of the word, but beneath his more somber exterior, he also had a generous, compassionate heart and a witty sense of humor.

"Are you enjoying the party?" he asked, facing the garden.

Ada turned in the same direction. "Truthfully, no. It has been nice to see old friends. However, in there . . ." She motioned to the house behind them. "I am Ada Thorne, rather than Ned's widow. Not one person has asked me tonight what happened to him or what has occupied my life for the past seven years."

Her words hung in the air between them, heavy with sorrow. But she didn't regret voicing them—not to Hugh, anyway.

"Next week will be an entire year since Ned was killed." She could hardly believe it. In some ways it seemed like yesterday, and in others, it felt like a lifetime had passed since she'd received that awful telegram. "One whole year since the Battle of the Somme."

Hugh nodded slowly. "It will be Harry's anniversary as well."

"Oh, Hugh, I'm sorry." She glanced at him in regret. "Here I am airing my grief when you have your own to manage."

His hand settled over hers where it rested on the balcony. The contact took her by surprise, but his touch was comforting, too. "There's no need for apology. Yes, I lost a brother, and that has been difficult. But I cannot imagine losing a spouse . . ."

"There are days I wake up, and for a moment, I forget that he isn't still off fighting. However, other days . . ." She let her voice trail out, afraid to continue.

Hugh gave her fingers a gentle squeeze, his gaze straight ahead. "Other days, you wonder if you're wrong for not missing them as keenly as you once did."

"That's it precisely," she said, relieved to feel understood.

Releasing her hand, he turned toward her, but his eyes seemed to be focused on something or someone from the past. "I went to France last year. To see how our boots were holding up and to check on Harry for my mother."

She hadn't known that. "You never mentioned you were there."

"I did not write that first letter until several months later."

Ada studied his troubled expression, wondering what he'd seen. "Would you tell me now what it was like?"

Hugh ran his hand over his clean-shaven face, drawing

her attention to his attire. He looked rather handsome in his evening clothes. "You truly wish to know?"

"Please. Ned shared so little."

"Very well." He exhaled a heavy sigh. "The first thing you notice is the smell. It is fouler than anything you can imagine, yet the soldiers pay it no mind. They go about their tasks in holes filled with disease, mud, and vermin, while the enemy lies in wait in his own filthy hole, intent on destroying you before you destroy him." His voice grew gruff with intensity. "I came quite close to a battlefield just once, but the quagmire of blood, death, and even more mud has haunted me since. I cannot imagine how anyone survives such a place."

It was Ada's turn to reach out. She placed her hand on the sleeve of his jacket. The reality of what he'd witnessed rested heavily on him, but she thought she detected a note of guilt beneath the horror.

"Do you wish you had gone to fight as they did?" She hoped he would not be angry at the personal inquiry.

He looked out over the garden again, his features thankfully devoid of offense. "At times, yes. Though I have tried to tell myself our brave boys need shoes for their feet, and I can provide those." Hugh glanced at her. "I believe it's been good for my mother to have one of us here as well."

"I agree," she said, smiling briefly. "You and I fight different battles than the soldiers, but I believe that is what God needs us to do."

Some of the tension faded from Hugh's demeanor. "Your husband told me nearly the same thing, when I saw him in France."

"You saw Ned?" Ada lowered her arm to her side. "And spoke with him?" A feeling of envy swept through her, despite its futility.

He mistook her words for concern. "If you'd rather I didn't speak of it."

"No, no. I'm merely jealous."

His eyebrows rose. "Of being in a war zone?"

"That is not what I meant," she said with a chuckle.

His mouth turned up in a half-smile before he became serious once more. "I'm sorry you weren't able to see and speak with him one final time, Ada. Ned talked of you and Rosemary that night. He even . . ."

"He even what?" she prompted.

Hugh faced her directly. "He asked me to look after the both of you if something were to happen to him, and I promised I would."

"Y-you did?" She felt a strange mixture of gratitude and confusion. "Is that why you wrote those letters and sent the Christmas gifts?" Had she been wrong in believing her and Hugh's renewed friendship was genuine? Had he merely been keeping his word and nothing more?

To her relief, he shook his head. "That was my reason for writing that first letter, yes, but everything after that was motivated by more than fulfilling a promise." He cleared his throat. "I continued writing because I rather enjoyed our letters."

Pleasure filled Ada at his admission. "I very much enjoyed them, too." Hoping to hide her embarrassment at saying so out loud, she changed the subject. "Was it nice to see Harry while you were there?"

"It was, and I will always cherish those hours." Hugh rested his hands on the balcony as Ada had earlier. "This war has certainly made a great mess of too many hearts."

"Yes, it has."

Neither of them spoke for another minute or so. But Ada felt no awkwardness in the silence, only shared grief and empathy between them.

"There you are, Ada."

She spun to face her mother, feeling strangely guilty at speaking with Hugh, alone. Though that was silly. They were old friends, after all. "Yes, Mamma?"

"Some of your guests are asking for you."

Ada nodded. "I'll be along in a moment."

"I will let them know." Her mother returned inside.

"If you'll excuse me, Hugh." Did she see her own disappointment at having to end their conversation reflected in his brown eyes? Or was she simply imagining it?

He motioned for her to go ahead. "I'll accompany you."

They started for the house, but they hadn't gone more than a few steps when he spoke again. "You can manage all this, Ada." Hugh waved his hand in the direction of the terrace doors. "After all, you survived the loss of your husband and the reality of nearly losing your daughter."

"I suppose that's true." Fresh confidence filled her at his words. "Thank you for your honesty just now, about the war."

"I will always be honest with you." His tone held no levity.

"I know, and I am grateful for it." They resumed walking. "Will you be staying longer?"

He appeared regretful as he said, "No, Mamma mentioned before I stepped outside that she was feeling tired."

Remorse filled her once more. "I'm glad you came. I hope to see much more of you . . ." Realizing how that might sound, she hurried to add, "You and your mother."

"We would both enjoy that," he said, giving her a rare full smile.

As Ada led him to the drawing room so she might say good night to Helena, she realized her headache had completely vanished, along with her hesitation about the party.

The night had not turned out as unbearable as she'd

expected, especially the last thirty minutes. And she had Hugh to thank for that.

September 1917

"Please stop pacing about, Ada," Victoria said, her words clipped. "You will make us dizzy."

Ada ended her circumference of the room at the window, where she drew aside the curtains. There were still several hours to go before supper would be served. "I'm sorry, Mamma. It's just that there is so little to . . ." She let the rest of her sentence fade into silence—she was in no mood for another lecture on the privilege of leisure.

If she read any more books or played the piano in the music room one more time, she might scream. She'd only been back at Stonefield Hall for six weeks, but she felt restless and unproductive during the hours Rosemary was at school.

Ada kept up her daily walks to visit Minnie. But now that her friend was working as Gran's cook, she had less time to talk than before. Even Hugh hadn't come around as much as Ada had hoped. She had seen him at church, and she, Rosemary, and Victoria had dined at Whitmore House twice. However, on each occasion, there'd been little time to converse privately with him.

"Would you care to go for a walk, pet?" she asked Rosemary, who sat on the sofa beside Victoria. Ada's mother was teaching her daughter needlework.

Rosemary glanced up. "No, thank you, Mummy. I want to keep sewing."

"Very well." Ada crossed the room toward the door. "I shall go and be back before supper."

"Did you not already go for a walk today?" Victoria called after her.

Ada turned and forced a smile. "Yes, but I believe another might be in order."

Slipping into the hall, she was relieved her mother didn't detain her with more questions. She'd quickly learned that her parents did not understand, nor did they wish to, about her life in London. An upper-class woman like her mother could not relate with the restlessness Ada felt here in the country.

There were days she dreamed of returning to her position at the paper warehouse, if only for something to do for herself and the war effort. In contrast, her parents seemed determined to pretend there wasn't a war going on—that everything at Stonefield Hall, particularly now that Ada had returned, would be exactly as it had always been.

She put on her hat and gloves as she exited the house. Which direction to walk? She considered taking out one of the horses for a ride. Except she'd prefer having someone along for company when she rode a horse for the first time in seven years.

Perhaps Hugh would be willing to accompany her if she asked. Cheered by the possibility, she set out for Whitmore House. The early evening air felt invigorating, something she couldn't say for London. If only she could find some cause or activity to fill her time.

When she arrived at the Whittingtons' home, the butler led her inside and down the hall to Hugh's study, where Ada waited outside the door.

"Mrs. Ada Henley to see you, sir," she heard the man announce.

Ada nodded approvingly—he'd spoken her name correctly.

"You may show her in," Hugh replied.

Giving the butler a grateful smile as he stepped back from the door, she entered the study. Hugh stood up from behind his desk.

"This is a pleasant surprise." His evident delight at seeing her eased some of the nervousness she suddenly felt at calling on him unexpectedly. "Please, have a seat."

She sat in the chair opposite the desk. "Thank you."

"To what do I owe this pleasure?" he asked, sitting down again.

Ada glanced at her hands. "I wondered if perhaps you might consider . . . coming on a ride . . . with me." Why did she feel tongue-tied, when she hadn't the night of her parents' party? "We could go this evening before supper." She forced her gaze upward to meet his. "Or another day this week."

"I would very much enjoy that, however . . ." His mouth flattened. "I'm afraid my time is not my own for another week or two." He waved a hand at several stacks of paper on his desk. "My secretary, Mr. Bertrup, was no longer exempt from enlisting and left to fight."

Ada felt more than a prick of disappointment that Hugh couldn't come, but it fled as she studied the exhausted lines on his face. "How long have you been without a secretary?"

"I'm not sure." He rubbed his forehead and pushed out a weary sigh. "Three weeks? Four, maybe? I've largely been able to crack on by myself, but only because I bring much of the paperwork and correspondence home from the factory each day."

A sudden notion had her leaning forward with excitement. It was the perfect solution to both their quandaries. "I could work as your secretary, at least until you're able to find a replacement."

"What?" Hugh chuckled as he shook his head. "I can't ask you to do that."

Ada shot him an arched look. "Why ever not? Is it because I am a woman?"

"Not at all," he said, looking uncomfortable. "I happen to employ a great many women at the boot factory."

This was a brilliant plan, if she could just get him to see it as such. "I'm quite good with numbers and correspondence."

"I'm sure you are . . ."

"Besides, you're not asking, Hugh. I'm offering."

He sat back in his chair, his expression conflicted. "You do not have to do this, Ada. I can manage on my own."

"I don't doubt that for a moment." She rested her clasped hands on top of the desk. "You've been managing on your own since you were twenty."

A flicker of pain she hadn't expected entered his brown eyes before he glanced away.

"What I mean," she hurried to explain, "is that you have been a great help to a great many people in your life, including myself. But who helps you?"

Hugh frowned. "Have you been plotting with my mother?"

"Your mother?" Ada echoed with a laugh. "No. Should I?"

His mouth lifted slightly at the corners. "Never mind. Are you certain you wish to do this?"

"Absolutely. You'll have the help you need, and I will have something to do." She lowered her voice to a loud whisper. "In truth, you would be helping me. If I don't have something to do soon, I am liable to go mad."

He deepened his smile. "Well, we can't have that, can we?" She watched the play of hesitation, understanding, and acceptance cross his countenance before he exhaled. "Very well. You're hired."

"That's wonderful." She eagerly rose to her feet. "Thank you."

Hugh stood as well. "Keep in mind, I insist on paying you wages."

"But I don't need—"

"That is my one stipulation."

This time, she eyed him with momentary indecision. The money wasn't necessary now that she was back at Stonefield, but if that was the only way to help him and herself, she would capitulate on the wages. "Fine. I accept."

"Excellent." He rounded his desk. "Why don't you come to the factory tomorrow morning, once Rosemary leaves for school?"

Ada followed him to the door. "I will."

"I do appreciate your willingness to help," he said quietly, pausing with his hand on the doorjamb. "And what you said a moment ago. I don't wish to be so prideful that I can't see I also need assistance now and again."

Standing this close, she was struck by the deep russet color of his eyes and the fine-looking lines of his jaw. A memory flitted through her mind. Something her maid, Hetty, had once said long ago, about Hugh being the handsomer of the two Whittington brothers. Ada had to admit she agreed with that sentiment.

Her cheeks heated at her errant thoughts and the curious way Hugh was watching her. "It often requires as much strength to ask for help," she said into the silence, "as it does to carry on."

"True enough." He opened the door for her, thankfully widening the distance between them. "I will see you tomorrow morning."

Ada nodded and returned his smile. "I shall be there."

She couldn't wait to tell Minnie and Gran about her new

job. Perhaps one of them would have an idea of how she might break the news to her parents, who would not be pleased. Whatever their reaction, though, Ada was looking forward to tomorrow for the first time in weeks.

Chapter 17

Hugh arrived earlier than usual at the factory the next morning to make certain his office and Mr. Bertrup's desk were as tidy as he could make them, in preparation for Ada's first day as his secretary. He still hadn't decided if her offer to help was a godsend or not. The idea of seeing her each workday was appealing, yet he hoped their friendship could remain the same, even if he was now her employer.

"Good morning."

He glanced up to find her smiling at him from the doorway. Like most of the women in the village these days, her dress of muted blue looked worn. But Hugh still thought her as pretty as ever, and he admired her for not purchasing a new wardrobe after returning home. He could well imagine what Victoria Thorne had to say about Ada's attire.

"Hello." As Hugh stood up from his chair, he glanced at the clock. "You are right on time."

Ada shrugged, though her dark eyes sparkled. "It's hard to break some habits. Being late to the warehouse would have cost me my position, so I learned for the first time in my life what it means to be punctual."

"Your desk is the one right outside the office." He crossed to the door. "Once you've looked it over, we might take a tour of the factory, if you wish."

She nodded. "I would love a tour."

After she'd seen her desk and stowed away her hat and gloves, she followed him through the factory's main rooms. Hugh introduced her to the foreman, Mr. Nelson, a man in his fifties who'd been in the same position under Hugh's father. The man's trusted council had been an asset for years, specifically during the first ones, when Hugh was learning how to run a factory.

The familiar hum of machinery filled the air. It was a sound Hugh often heard in his dreams. A number of the women employees eyed him and Ada with open curiosity. Several whispered to those seated behind them. Hugh didn't mind them talking as long as they completed their work.

"It's quite impressive," Ada said when they returned to her desk. "I had no idea you could produce so many boots in a single day."

He smiled at the compliment. "I couldn't do it alone. Our workers are efficient and turn out good quality."

"It may help that some of them are a bit enamored with the factory owner." Her gaze brightened with amusement.

Hugh pocketed his hands, feeling uneasy. "I don't believe that is true."

"No?" She shot him an impish smile. "I observed more than one pair of eyes following you about the room. Then there was all the whispering."

Had those women been discussing him? He shifted his weight. "All of them have acted with proper decorum, and I'm grateful for their extraordinary work ethic."

"So no sweetheart among them for you?"

He cleared his throat. "No."

"Was there ever someone?" Ada tilted her head and regarded him seriously. "I can't recall."

At once, the room felt too warm and confining. Hugh had promised to be honest with her, but there was no point in dredging up old history, either.

"I did care for someone once," he replied truthfully. "But I did not speak soon enough to win her heart, and then I became busy running this place." He unpocketed his hand and waved at the room.

"I imagine that hurt. To have lost a chance like that."

It was time to change the subject. "I can explain what I remember of Mr. Bertrup's responsibilities, but feel free to ask me any questions that may arise."

"I will." She took a seat at her desk. "And thank you, Hugh."

He raised his eyebrows in silent question.

"For the position and for sharing what you did just now." She studied him, her expression open and earnest.

Words he'd stopped himself from saying years ago settled on his tongue, anxious for release. "I . . ." It required great self-discipline from him to swallow back the futile statements. But swallow them he did.

"You're most welcome." His smile was more than a little forced, though Ada didn't seem to notice.

He'd voiced as much of the truth regarding the past as he planned to. Now it was time to focus once more on the present.

It took Ada several weeks to master all of her secretarial duties, but once she did, she found she enjoyed her new position far more than the one at the warehouse. Of course, it also helped that Hugh was her manager, and as such, she was able to see him more frequently than she had before coming to work at the factory.

While she still considered him a good friend, when at work, she did her best to keep things professional between them. That meant eating lunch with the other women and always referring to Hugh as "*Mr. Whittington" in their presence.*

True to her predictions on her first day, she'd learned a fair portion of the young ladies at the factory found Hugh quite handsome, though more of them found his somber nature less appealing. Ada didn't divulge the information that she and Hugh had known each other for years or that she would have once agreed with their assessment of him. Now she knew differently. She'd seen a side to Hugh, both through his letters and since her return to Yorkshire, that she realized most people didn't, and that knowledge made her feel as if she possessed a rare gift.

Her parents had finally ceased their protests about her employment—and she had Hugh's mother to thank for that. On her second day at the factory, Ada had confided their reaction to Hugh, who had apparently spoken of it to Helena. She had then paid a call to Ada's mother, and while there had extolled her gratitude toward Ada for stepping in to help her son and had thus pacified Charles and Victoria.

Ada relished feeling useful again, something that not even Minnie or her grandmother could completely understand. However, she suspected Hugh did. Her favorite time of day was riding home with him in his family's automobile. It was then that they could simply be themselves—not just secretary and employer—and talk openly.

One autumn afternoon after she'd returned home from

the factory, she found their butler, Stewart, waiting for her. "There's a visitor to see you, Mrs. Henley."

"To see me?"

Rosemary ran up to give Ada a hug, and she listened to the girl's account of her school day for a minute or two. When her daughter skipped off to the library, Ada turned to the butler again. "Who is the visitor, Stewart?"

"It's your father's solicitor, Mr. Peckering. I put him in the study."

Ada threw a look at the study door. "And you're certain he wishes to see me? Not my father?"

"Correct, ma'am."

She wasn't entirely surprised by this news. Her father was now confined to his room day and night.

"The gentleman was quite adamant," the butler added. "Insisted he would wait until your return."

Wariness at the solicitor's purpose for coming churned in Ada's stomach. "Thank you, Stewart. I will see him now."

As she entered her father's study, a thin, balding man rose to his feet to greet her. "Ada Henley," she said, offering her hand.

"Terrence Peckering." He gave her fingers a weak shake.

Ada indicated he return to his seat as she took hers behind the desk. "How may I help you, Mr. Peckering?"

"First, may I express my regret at hearing how ill your father has become."

She offered a tight smile. "Thank you. Is that why you asked to meet with me?"

"It is, Mrs. Henley." His gaze skittered away, then back. "I bring rather unpleasant news that would no doubt be difficult for your father to hear or comprehend at present."

His statement only added to her mounting concern, but Ada nodded for him to continue. He pulled a sheaf of papers from his bag and began to explain the purpose of his visit in rather rapid tones. It was as if he feared she might stop him or throw him out before he had a chance to finish.

By the time Mr. Peckering sat back in his chair, visibly spent, Ada didn't blame him for his earlier worries. Had she known beforehand what news he brought, she might have refused to listen to him.

"I'd like to be certain I understand you, Mr. Peckering." She managed to keep her voice calm, though dread pulsed inside her. At his nod, she continued. "I am the heiress to this estate, upon my father's death, per his will and because Stonefield Hall is not entailed."

"That is correct."

The next words were harder to push from her constricted throat. "However, you are also here to inform me that we have no money."

"I wouldn't say *no money,* Mrs. Henley." He appeared as ill at ease as Ada felt, but she found scant comfort in that fact. "It is more a matter of having *little money.*"

She pressed her lips over a retort about the minute difference between having no money and little money. But she reminded herself that this man wasn't to blame for the troubling information he'd brought her.

Why had her father concealed from her their precarious financial situation? Why had her mother thrown such an elaborate party for Ada's return when the estate was barely limping along? She could guess the answer, at least in part. For Charles and Victoria, appearances, reputation, and grandeur must be maintained, whether the coffers were full or nearly empty.

Well, no more.

"Can we economize?" she asked, breaking the silent tension in the room.

Mr. Peckering cleared his throat. "It will surely help, yes. You could let go of any extra staff, rule out entertaining altogether, and sell off any heirlooms or jewelry."

"However?" She hadn't missed the hesitation underlying his tone.

He coughed again. "If you cannot increase the productivity of the land, then it's only a matter of time before you will be forced to sell it piece by piece."

Sell parts of the estate? Ada pinched the bridge of her nose, where a headache was forming. This was her home—even if she'd only just returned. This was where she had met Ned and where her ancestors had resided for more than a hundred years. There had to be something more she could do.

"What do you know of my father's land agent?"

The solicitor shifted in his chair. She wasn't sure if he felt more uncomfortable discussing business with a woman or at bringing such tidings when her father was not long for this world. "The man is past his prime, I'm afraid. A younger, more modern-thinking fellow might bring about better results for the estate."

"I see."

Perhaps she could speak with Hugh and seek his advice. But Ada dismissed the idea straightaway. He would want to increase her wages at the factory, and she didn't want him feeling beholden or responsible for what was a private family matter.

When she stood, the solicitor did the same. "Thank you for your time and information, Mr. Peckering. Would you care for some tea before you go?"

He shook his head. "No, thank you, Mrs. Henley. I must get back."

"Another time, then. Thank you."

After a parting nod, he rushed from the room. Ada

slumped into her chair as the door clicked shut behind him. Was this why she'd been led to come home? To turn things around? In her time away from Stonefield, she'd certainly learned how to economize. Now it seemed those lessons might prove useful.

"What did Mr. Peckering want?" Victoria asked as she entered the study. "Did he come to see your father?"

Ada climbed to her feet. "No, Mamma, he specifically asked to see me."

"Whatever for?" She looked annoyed.

It was all Ada could do to hide her own annoyance at her parents' decisions, ones that now affected her and Rosemary and the future of Stonefield Hall. Yet how could she help her mother see that? There was a possibility Victoria knew as little as Ada had.

"Mr. Peckering met with me because he'd been informed that Papa's condition has grown worse." She approached her mother and scooped up her hand. Victoria glanced away, her eyes glittering with unshed tears. "As heiress to this estate after he is gone, I'm going to insist we make some changes."

"What sort of changes?" Victoria asked in a sharp tone.

Ada squeezed her hand. "Did you know about the trouble with the estate finances?"

"A bit." She waved her free hand dismissively. "However, your father said not to worry, and so I haven't."

"Papa has been indulgent." Ada waited for her mother to look her in the eye before she continued. "If we do nothing, we will have to sell off pieces of the land."

Victoria's face paled, then hardened. "Sell some of the estate? Never."

"I do not want that, either, Mamma, but it is going to require sacrifice if we are to avoid it." She released her mother's hand and strode out of the study.

"What sort of sacrifice?"

Ada moved toward the staircase that led to the basement and the servants' work areas. She hoped her forthcoming conversation with their housekeeper would go far better than the present one with her mother. "We will need to cut down on the number of staff we employ, trim back our meals, and eliminate all parties."

"You cannot be serious," Victoria said, clearly horrified.

"Quite serious. I will also be replacing Mr. Jockapeth with a new land agent. Hopefully, we can find money somewhere to give him a small pension so he can remain in his cottage."

Victoria stamped her foot in anger. The action reminded Ada of one of Rosemary's occasional tantrums. "This is too much, Ada. We will be the laughingstock of the neighborhood by the time you are through with us."

"That may be true, but at least we might still have a home."

She started down the stairs, but her mother's next hurled words stopped her descent. "You could marry, you know. Someone with money this time, someone who could actually save the estate and our way of life."

Resentment coursed through Ada. She clenched her hands into fists at her sides, yet she didn't turn.

"I do not plan to marry again," she said, tilting her chin higher. "But if I did, it would not be for money. It would be for love, as it was the first time. So we will simply have to practice frugality and hope it proves to be enough."

Chapter 18

No sooner had Ada, her mother, and Rosemary sat down to supper that evening than Stewart appeared. "Mrs. O'Reilly to see you, Mrs. Henley."

Victoria frowned, though Ada wasn't sure if it was because of Minnie's visit or at hearing her daughter constantly referred to by Ned's last name.

"Is William here, too?" Rosemary asked eagerly.

The butler shook his head. "I'm afraid she is alone, Miss Rosemary."

"Thank you, Stewart." Ada set down her napkin and exited the dining room. Why had Minnie walked over to Stonefield Hall, and at this hour? Normally, she waited for Ada to come see her at Gran's house, since in spite of Ada's best efforts, her mother had not warmed to her dear friends.

She found Minnie standing in the entryway, looking nervously about. "So good to see you, Minnie." Ada smiled. "I'm sorry I have not been by as frequently . . ." The pained look on her friend's face sent a jolt of fear through her. "What is it?"

"I got this today." She lifted a slip of paper—a telegram.

Crossing to Minnie's side in two strides, Ada took hold of her arms. "Is it Thomas? He hasn't been . . ." She couldn't say the rest.

"'E's . . . 'e's been wounded." Minnie's hand trembled as she lifted it to her mouth.

Ada hugged her tightly, relieved Thomas was alive. "Do you know the extent of his injuries?"

"Not yet," Minnie said when Ada released her. Several tears leaked from her green eyes. "But I'm scared, Ada. What if 'e's real bad off?"

"Have you told Gran?"

Nodding, Minnie wiped at her eyes. "She said we'll make it work, what with me likely needin' to care for 'im and cook, too."

Gratitude filled Ada at the news. Minnie and her family were in good hands with her grandmother to watch out for them. "Depending on what his injuries are, he might find work at the Whittingtons' boot factory. I could ask Hugh, if Thomas agrees to it."

"That's an idea." Minnie fell back a step. "I'll go now. Sorry to disturb your supper."

Ada gave her a stern look. "You never have to apologize for coming here. You are my friend, just as you've always been and always will be."

"Thank you," Minnie said with a tremulous smile. "I thought you'd want to know."

"Of course." Ada followed her outside. "I'll be praying for Thomas. Let me know when he is to arrive in Yorkshire and if there is anything I might do."

"I will. Night, Ada."

Lifting her hand in a wave, she echoed the sentiment. "Good night, Minnie."

She watched her friend walk down the drive, then turned

back toward the house. The estate's financial troubles and the additional news that Thomas had been wounded weighed heavily on her mind and heart, disrupting the relative calm of the last few months. Living in London, raising her daughter, and returning home after seven years weren't the only things that were going to require good courage.

Something was troubling Ada. She had gone straight to her desk that morning without her usual cheerful greeting. Hugh waited an agonizing ten minutes before he could no longer stand the silence.

"Morning," he said, exiting his office.

She glanced up and smiled, but the gesture lacked animation. "Good morning. Have you been here long?" While they rode home together each evening, the Thornes' driver brought Ada to the factory after Rosemary left for school in the mornings.

"Thirty minutes or so."

With a nod, she bent over her desk again.

"Is something amiss?" Looking around to ensure there was no one nearby, Hugh added quietly, "You seem rather sad today."

She lifted her head, giving him a glimpse at her dark eyes. They were indeed filled with pain. "I ..." She tapped her fingers against the desk, as if making a decision. He hoped she would share what was bothering her. "I learned yesterday that Minnie's husband, Thomas, has been wounded."

"I'm sorry to hear that." Hugh spoke regularly with Minnie and her children at church on Sundays. He liked the woman's kind, unpretentious nature. "That's rather horrid news."

Ada nodded. "I wish to help in some way, but I'm not sure how."

"I'm the least likely source for offering that kind of advice," he said, giving her a meaningful look.

The conversation in his study when she'd offered to be his secretary had proven to be one of many between them on the subject of helping others and being helped.

As he'd hoped, she laughed lightly. "I believe you might be the perfect source. I don't wish to overstep with Thomas, especially not knowing the extent of his injuries. But Minnie is as dear to me as a sister, and I want to do something."

"Prayer does wonders."

He could stand by that piece of advice. His sincere prayers had helped him after he'd learned all those years ago that Ada loved someone else, and more recently after his mother had lovingly counseled him to stop assuming responsibility for everyone. Since then, he'd been much more deliberate about allowing others to grow in their own way and to consider when he might offer help.

"One thing more," he added, remembering something his mother had shared with him the other day. "People often need a listening ear more than anything else. That's something you can offer both Minnie and Thomas."

Ada's smile was warm and genuine this time, and sent his heart jolting. "Wonderful advice, Hugh." Blushing, she peered cautiously around them. "I mean, Mr. Whittington."

"I believe you're safe from the factory spies."

She laughed fully. "Are you sure? One never knows when and where they might be lurking about."

Returning her smile, he moved toward his office. Inside, he dropped into his chair. With the way his pulse was crashing about, he felt as if he'd jogged to the factory instead of simply dispensed advice.

What would Ada say if she knew he looked forward to seeing her each day? Or that she was a constant in his thoughts when they were apart? Or that the feelings he'd once felt for her had begun to return, only deeper?

"No," Hugh growled, straightening.

He would keep their friendship as it was for as long as he possibly could.

Ada had hoped to go with Minnie to the train station to meet Thomas, but he'd requested little fanfare or a crowd. So after two days had passed, she set out for the O'Reilly cottage to see if Thomas was up to receiving visitors yet. She left a much-disappointed Rosemary at home, but she felt certain Minnie's husband would not want another child about, eyeing him curiously. Minnie had shared Thomas's last letter with Ada, in which he'd delivered the news that he had lost his left leg below the knee.

The children were playing out in front of the cottage and greeted Ada as she walked up. "Is your mother in or at Gran's?"

"She's inside," Janey answered. "Are you here to see Daddy?"

Ada nodded.

"He's still sad." The ten-year-old girl frowned. "Though Mama says that's normal."

Compassion for their family, Thomas most of all, prevented Ada from replying for a moment. "I believe your mother is right. Your papa has experienced a great deal."

"He cried when he saw me." Janey looked up at Ada. "But he said it weren't because he was sad. It was 'cause he was so happy."

She ran her hand down the girl's golden red hair. "I imagine he was quite happy and very surprised with how big you have grown."

"I'm big, too," seven-year-old William announced with self-importance as he joined them.

Ada laughed. "Yes, you are."

After a brief knock on the cottage door, she walked inside, calling out, "Minnie?" It reminded her so much of London that a wave of nostalgia washed over her.

"'Ello, Ada," Minnie called back, her tone cheerful but weary. "I'm in the kitchen, just puttin' together a cold supper."

Ada wandered into the kitchen. It was a large, bright room with a range, similar to the one they'd both had in their flats in the city. Her reminiscence swelled to gratitude that Minnie and her family had come to Yorkshire, too.

"How is he?" she asked softly.

A pained expression passed over Minnie's face as she arranged some cheese on a plate. "'E's all right. Alive, praise the Lord. I think 'e's still 'urtin' more inside than out." She looked at Ada, her eyes watery with tears. "But it's been a bit better since I told 'im I weren't going nowhere. Yelled at 'im, actually. I told 'im I'll love 'im no matter what's 'appened to 'im. Or what 'e's seen."

She could easily recall when Minnie's heartfelt goading had helped Ada through her own grief. "I imagine he didn't take too kindly to your methods at first, but he's probably feeling grateful now."

"Oh, 'e was angry all right—we both were." Minnie shot her an impish smile. "Then we were crying and 'olding each other."

"Would he welcome a visit?" Ada glanced over her shoulder in the direction of the stairs.

Her friend dried her hands on her apron and moved

toward the outer door. "'E's out back. In the garden. I'll tell 'im you're 'ere." She slipped out the door, shutting it behind her.

Ada waited, her stomach knotting with nerves. Though she'd known Thomas for years, she wasn't entirely sure how one ought to act or talk to a wounded soldier. Then Hugh's remark from the other day returned to her thoughts. If Thomas wished to talk, she could offer him a listening ear.

"'E says to go on through."

Smiling, Ada joined Minnie by the door.

"Thank you for comin' to see 'im." Her friend gave her arm a grateful squeeze.

She nodded. "I'll come back inside before I leave."

The shade felt cool as Ada exited the cottage and walked the short distance to where Thomas sat in one of two chairs situated on the grass. He rose, with the aid of a cane, as she approached.

"Hello, Ada."

She took his hand when he offered it and squeezed it between her own. "It's wonderful to see you, Thomas."

"Please . . ." He motioned to the empty chair beside him. Once she was situated, he dropped into his own chair and set the cane beside him on the ground. "I was right sorry to hear about Ned." Thomas shook his head, frowning. "T'weren't a better man."

Ada felt a sting of grief. "I appreciate you saying so. How are you faring?"

"Can't complain too much," he said with a sniff. "Most of me mates in our station lost more'n their legs. At least I'm back with me family. They won't see theirs again in this life."

The anguish behind his words and in his voice brought a lump to Ada's throat. "I'm so sorry. Ned would write and tell me how close he was to those he fought alongside. How they were almost like brothers to him." She couldn't imagine witnessing the death of so many close friends.

"Aye. That we were."

She finally glanced at his pant leg. It had been hemmed below his left knee. Beyond that, there was nothing. *More loss,* she thought sadly.

"Will you tell me about them?"

"Who?" Thomas glanced at her as if he'd forgotten she was there. Perhaps he had.

She leaned against the back of the chair. "About your mates and what happened to them . . . about what happened to you."

"Some of that weren't fit for a lady to hear."

"I'll not argue with you there," she said as she met his gaze. "But I would like to hear some of it."

Thomas stared down at his hands. "Minnie keeps sayin' I need to share it." He gave a shake of his head, a brief smile touching his lips. "What I wouldn't do for that woman." He visibly swallowed. "I love her with all my breath."

"And she loves you."

"Aye, even when she's ahollerin' at me." He smirked, but his hazel eyes shone with pure affection.

Some of Ada's wistfulness returned. She remembered times when Ned had looked at her that way, and she missed it.

"While I have not been the recipient of her hollering," Ada admitted after a moment, "I was rather angry with her last year when she called me a coward."

"Did she now?" He looked as surprised as he was amused.

"She was right, too." Ada wanted him to know she'd also struggled with feeling her grief, with sharing it. "I was cowardly in refusing to talk about how I felt after Ned was killed. I kept it all bottled up inside." She gazed out over the garden. "Not until I finally told her everything could I breathe again."

Thomas shifted in his chair. "Are you tellin' me all this so I'll talk?"

"Yes." She tempered her answer with a smile. "However, if you don't wish to talk, I'll not blame you one bit. I certainly didn't want to share anything at first."

Lifting his chin, he peered up at the clouds meandering across the sky. Ada wondered if he would keep silent. She wouldn't judge him if he did. There were things she suspected Hugh hadn't told her about his time in France, and he hadn't been there as a solider.

"I s'pose I might tell you some," he said after a moment. "But only some, mind you." He wagged his finger at her. "Ned'll come back to haunt me if I share it all."

That made her chuckle. "I'll listen to whatever you wish to share."

Thomas paused again. Ada guessed he was gathering his thoughts, sifting through what he could and couldn't give voice to. At last, he released a weighty sigh and began. "There were four of us mates. Me, MacDonald, Perrish, and Clompton..."

Ada lost track of time as she listened to his stories. Some of them made her laugh, others had her biting her lip to keep from crying out in horror. Then there were the tales that left her silently weeping, especially when he revealed that none of his three friends had survived the battle that cost Thomas his leg.

"That's enough for now," he said sometime later, throwing her a chagrined look.

She brushed at her damp eyes with her thumb. "Thank you, Thomas."

"Aye. You've been a dear friend to me and mine for years, Ada Henley." His next words came out slightly choked. "And you took care of me Minnie while I was away."

Several more tears spilled onto her cheeks. "She took just as much care of me."

"Either way, I'm grateful."

Ada rose from her chair. "If you recall other stories you wish to share, I would like to hear them. It helps me, too." She glanced down at the grass. "Even with Ned gone, I feel close to him when I can better understand what he experienced."

"Well, we'll see," Thomas hedged, though his hopeful expression told a different tale. "Thanks for comin' by."

With a wave, she turned and headed toward the cottage. Listening to Thomas's accounts of the war had drained her of energy, yet she felt ironically buoyed up at the same time.

Minnie and Hugh had both been right—talking out one's grief did loosen the burden, and not just for the one grieving. Ada entered the O'Reillys' home less troubled in her own heart than when she had arrived.

Chapter 19

October 1917

THE LEADEN CLOUDS dripped rain, forming rivulets of water that ran into the fresh hole in the cemetery. Ada stared at her father's casket. The rest of the funeral attendees, including her mother, grandmother, and Rosemary, had wandered over to the church gate, their umbrellas framing somber faces and hushed voices. But Ada couldn't move. The moment she did, she would have to accept that her life had irrevocably changed—yet again.

While she'd once loathed her father's silence, she'd also found comfort in the belief that he and Stonefield Hall would always be there. Now he was gone, and if she couldn't turn things around with the estate, their home might soon be gone, too.

Footsteps sounded to her right. It was probably the gravediggers, but she wasn't ready to leave. Seconds turned to minutes as she stared at the clots of dirt she and her mother had thrown onto the casket below.

The responsibility of the estate—and its frightening

financial situation—had officially fallen onto her shoulders the moment her father had taken his last breath. Ada lowered her head as the weight of those duties pressed with renewed heaviness upon her, the brim of her hat weeping with raindrops.

"Ada?" Hugh said, touching her lightly on the elbow. She peered up at his face. "The gravediggers are saying they need to finish before the rain grows worse."

She eyed the pair of men standing at a respectful distance with chagrin. "Oh, yes. Of course." Glancing back at the grave, she bid a silent goodbye to her father.

Hugh fell into step beside her as she traversed the path through the wet grass and gravestones toward the gate. But the sight of all those people waiting to offer their condolences created a stir of panic inside her.

"I-I'm not ready to go just yet. Will you see if my mother and Gran will take Rosemary home? I'll walk back in a bit." She turned to face the old stone church. "I want more time inside."

She felt Hugh's gaze on her. "I'll speak with them. My mother may wish to go now as well. Let me drive you home, though. Whenever you are ready."

Some of her anxiety slipped away in the wake of his kindness. "Thank you." Averting her gaze from the crowd of mourners, she hurried back inside the church. The cool air felt surprisingly soothing. The priest was still outside with the others, which meant she had the place to herself for the moment.

Selecting a middle pew this time, Ada took a seat on the hard wooden bench. She unpinned her sodden hat and placed it beside her to dry. At last, she was able to draw a full breath, one laden with the scent of candle wax. The tightness in her chest began to loosen.

She felt so very tired. Watching her father's health deteriorate completely, working as Hugh's secretary, and doing what small things she could think of to save the estate had all taken their toll. She longed to sleep for days.

The church door creaked open, alerting her that someone had come inside. Ada frowned. She wanted more time alone. The footfalls neared, and she lifted her chin to see Hugh approaching. Her irritation gave way to relief. She didn't mind Hugh's presence right now. He sat beside her on the pew, but he remained, thankfully, silent.

Ada gazed about the church, stopping on the stained-glass window at her left. It was a beautiful depiction of Christ raising Jairus's daughter from the dead. When Ada had come across the story in her reading, she'd read it through over and over again.

How well she could relate to the man's grief at losing his daughter. And then to see the girl alive and whole, as Ada had Rosemary that summer day at the school. Tears pricked her eyes at the memory.

What intense pain Jairus must have felt, pain Ada herself had felt this last year, before the miracle occurred of seeing his daughter's life restored. Yet it was that heartache and grief that had led the man to seek Jesus. The same pattern had proven true in Ada's life. Each painful experience had been an opportunity to seek God and to grow, even if she hadn't always recognized it as such.

"Coming home was the right thing to do," she admitted into the stillness. "I knew that for certain after learning how ill my father had become. Yet everything has been rather different from what I expected." She turned to peer at Hugh. "I thought I would have more time with him. And in spite of everything . . ." Her voice hitched with emotion as tears dampened her dry eyes. "I will miss him."

Instead of speaking, he simply scooted closer and tugged her toward him. Ada willingly went, weeping against his rain-splattered coat. She was trying so hard to be courageous. But today, in this moment, she needed someone else's strength to lean on.

"Of course you will miss him," he said in a low voice a few minutes later. "It's never easy to lose a parent, especially after so short a reconciliation."

Ada sniffled and brushed at her wet cheeks, but she didn't sit up. In Hugh's embrace, she felt protected, comforted. "My parents never wrote while I was in London—not once." A shadow of the pain she'd felt at finding that first unopened letter after her miscarriage fluttered through her. "I wrote a handful of times, but my letters were returned, unopened. After Rosemary was six months old, I decided it was best to stop trying."

"Their silent disregard for you never did sit right with me."

She inched back in surprise. "You knew about that?"

"I did," Hugh said, his brow furrowed.

"You didn't speak of it in your letters."

He turned to face the front of the church. "Believe me, I wished to, particularly when they came to dine or Mamma and I visited Stonefield Hall. But I didn't feel it my place to say something. I only mentioned it now because . . ." Hugh looked at her again, his smile sad. "Because I understand today must be doubly hard for you. To have so many years of heartache followed by so short a reprieve."

"Thank you." It pleased her to know Hugh hadn't condoned her parents' past actions. "Did your mother leave with mine?"

He nodded.

"Helena will be a great comfort to her." Hugh's mother understood what it was like to lose a husband.

Hugh twisted on the bench to face her. "What of you? Who will be your comfort?"

Ada could recall asking a similar question of him. And though she guessed he meant the words to be playful, the look in his brown eyes was strikingly serious.

"You've been a great comfort to me, and more than just today."

He rested his arm along the back of the pew. And though he didn't touch her, she felt the warmth of his nearness, and it caused her pulse to trip in a strangely new and pleasant way.

"I'm glad to hear it," he said, his mouth twitching with a hidden smile. "However, that's only if I have not been foisting that help upon you."

The friendly banter between them was familiar territory, and Ada seized hold of it. "Perhaps just once or twice."

He laughed. "I see that as an improvement."

"As you should." She gave him a full smile. His friendship meant the world to her, and she appreciated his honesty as much as his teasing. A prick of guilt speared her at the realization she hadn't been completely honest with him in return. "I do have a confession to make."

"Sounds intriguing," he said lightly. "And appropriate given the setting."

"Do you remember last month when you asked if something was amiss, and I told you about Minnie's husband?"

Hugh appeared momentarily confused, then he nodded. "I remember."

"That was not the only thing on my mind."

"Ada ..." The note of disappointment in his voice increased her regret.

She stared straight ahead, not wishing to see his expression until after she'd shared the truth. "Earlier that same evening, I had a visit from my father's solicitor. Apparently, the estate is in great financial trouble."

"Are you serious?"

She answered with a nod. "My father has been rather indulgent, and while my mother knew the situation in part, she didn't understand the full extent. Even knowing it now, she refuses to believe we must make changes if we want to keep the estate intact."

"The estate is not entailed, is it?"

"No, and now that my father is gone, I have the final say on what we do."

When Hugh remained silent, she went on, eager to unburden herself to someone who wouldn't balk at the changes she'd either made or proposed. "I've already let go of some of the staff and have been hoping to find a new land agent, but I know so little about farming. I don't wish to sell any part of Stonefield. However, I fear that may be inevitable."

She studied her gloved hands as she thought of all the tasks they'd been required to do during her time in London. "It's a shame, really, that everything cannot be solved by simply thinning the soup or doing our own laundry or trading goods with our neighbors." Her laugh held more irony than amusement. "Those things were—are—still second nature to me."

Ada regarded Hugh again. He was watching her with a sorrowful expression that squeezed at her heart. "Why didn't you tell me sooner about the estate? I thought we were . . ." He frowned. "We are friends, are we not?"

"Yes," she said earnestly, "the very best of friends."

His frown increased. "Then why keep this to yourself? I could have raised your salary a month ago."

"That is exactly why I did not want to tell you." Agitated, as much with him as with herself, she stood and moved down the bench to stare out the nearest window.

She heard him give a disgruntled sniff. "Who is being stubborn now? We both know that strength is not about refusing help."

"I was embarrassed, Hugh," she shot back. "And angry. Even now, I cannot believe they let things become so bad. I had hoped to save things on my own, so yes, I was being stubborn. But I don't wish to be—not anymore."

The sound of his footsteps moving toward her echoed through the quiet church, yet Ada didn't turn. She heard him stop behind her, then his hands wrapped gently around her shoulders. "I don't blame you for your embarrassment or anger. I only wish you'd been honest with me sooner."

Tears blurred her eyes as he slowly spun her to face him. "I'm sorry."

"All is forgiven," Hugh said in a sincere tone. "And if you absolutely insist, I will not raise your salary."

She managed a wobbly smile. "I do insist, but I know of another way you can help. If you're willing."

"Anything."

"I wish to hear your opinion on something our land agent suggested. He believes we need to drain a sizeable section of the estate to ensure better crops. Unfortunately, it will cost a great deal of funds to accomplish."

"I'm much more an expert on boots and running a factory than I am regarding land, but we made some improvements to our estate a few years ago that have helped." He lowered his hands to his sides. "What if I asked my land agent to visit Stonefield? I trust the chap's opinion."

Relief washed through her. "That would be wonderful."

"I do have one stipulation." A teasing glint lit his brown eyes.

Ada couldn't help a laugh. "Oh, dear. Not that again. What is it this time?"

"Not your wages, I promise."

"Good. Then I'm listening."

The mischievousness disappeared from his face. "We have yet to take that horse ride you suggested the other month."

"This is true." The fact that he'd remembered her invitation filled her with pleasure. "Is that your stipulation, then? You will help me if I agree to go riding with you?"

He gave a decisive nod. "Yes."

"I might be rather slow and awkward. It has been years."

His full smile animated her pulse again. "I'm certain you will have no difficulty remembering how to ride as well as ever."

"Then it's settled." She indicated he precede her down the bench. "How soon would you and your land agent be able to visit? And when do you wish to go riding?" Picking up her hat, she followed him down the aisle.

Hugh considered the question. "How about Saturday next for both?"

"I would like that," she said, feeling anticipation as well as peace as they exited the church.

Ada reined in her horse, then turned to look over her shoulder at Hugh and his mount, still a ways behind. A full-throated laugh escaped her lips. She'd forgotten how much she loved riding, and that realization had come too late. Next week, equestrian buyers would descend upon Stonefield Hall to purchase the estate's horses, though to Ada's great relief, Hugh had asked to buy her father's stallion.

"Your riding is neither awkward nor slow," he joked as

he stopped his horse alongside hers. The animal danced to the side at the sudden change in speed.

She laughed again. "Thank you for indulging me in a race."

"My pleasure." The sincerity in his eyes made her pulse tumble erratically, as it had the other week when they'd spoken inside the church. "I didn't doubt for a moment that your riding skills would return."

"So they have." She nudged her horse in the direction of Whitmore House, and Hugh fell in beside her. "I only wish I'd thought to teach Rosemary how to ride before making the decision to sell the horses."

He glanced at her. "Rosemary is welcome to ride any of our horses. Either myself or our stable master would be more than willing to teach her."

"She would love that." Ada smiled to show her earnestness. "Thank you."

Her daughter had followed Hugh about earlier that day, when he and his land agent had visited the estate. Ada suspected it was partly because Rosemary missed her grandfather, and partly because Hugh never showed annoyance at her persistent, curious questions. He always answered them with patience. Rosemary had been visibly disappointed when the tour of the estate had ended.

"Have you decided what you will do with your land?" he asked.

Ada nodded—she'd decided not long after the men had left that afternoon. "The advice of your land agent seems sound. I will sell some of the land, as he suggested, and use the money to fund the draining of the other fields."

"I wish you did not have to sell any part of it." His gaze moved to Whitmore House in the distance. "It's your home."

Her carefree mood wilted at the reminder. "I feel the

same, but I believe we will be fine." She shifted in the saddle and straightened her shoulders. "I'm certain God did not send me here for naught. He has something in mind for me and Rosemary, whether or not I understand what it is at present."

"There are plenty of people who care deeply for you and are ready to help in whatever capacity you wish."

The conviction behind his words and the intensity of his expression as he looked her way stole the moisture from her mouth. Did Hugh care deeply for her in the same way that Minnie or her grandmother did? Ada wasn't sure, and a part of her feared knowing the answer.

"I appreciate your assistance today," she said with sincerity. "And if you or your land agent have any other solutions, I would be most grateful to hear them."

A comfortable silence settled between them before Hugh spoke again. "I have one other solution. However, I'm sure you will not like it."

"Why ever not? I wish to save as much of the estate as I can." When he hesitated further, she shot him an impatient look. "Please, Hugh."

"Very well." He faced forward again. "If you were to marry a man of means, your new husband would be able to assist in saving the estate."

Shock and a modicum of panic kept her from replying straightaway. How ironic that his suggestion would so closely mirror her mother's for saving Stonefield Hall.

"I did warn you that you would not like this particular solution."

Ada cleared her throat and threw him a weak smile. "You were correct."

"I meant no offense..."

"I understand. And yes, a marriage such as that would help far more than anything I'm doing or intend to do.

But . . ." Tilting her chin upward, she hoped he would respect her resolve on this subject. "I will not marry for money as my parents did. They may have shared affection for each other, but there was never a deep, resounding love between them." Not as there'd been between her and Ned.

When Hugh said nothing, she asked, "Did your parents marry for money?"

"I believe that was one of the reasons for their union, yes."

Ada had to work hard to hide her smugness. "I chose not to marry for money once, and should I marry a second time, it would still not be for financial gain."

"I admire your convictions—to a point."

"To a point?" she echoed.

Hugh raised his eyebrows. "I did promise to be honest with you."

So he had, and she was grateful for that honesty—most of the time. Ada released her breath in an attempt to calm herself. How had they ended up pursuing such a topic, anyway?

"Which point do you disagree with?"

"Not disagree per se." He sent her a playful smile that tempered her frustration. "I only wished to share a different possibility, which you may have not considered." She nodded for him to continue. "My parents did marry for money, but they also married because they loved each other."

Ada tried to recall what she'd observed in the interactions between Helena and Hugh's father before the man's death. But she had been a child at the time and couldn't remember any specific details. Clearly, they'd had a different relationship than her parents had.

"There are times when one does not have to choose between love and wealth." His direct look had the power to command her heartbeat. "Sometimes, as in the case of my parents, one is able to have both."

For the second time in so many minutes, Ada found herself unable to respond. Was there more to Hugh's words than she wanted to believe?

He was her dearest friend as well as a benevolent employer. There had also been moments recently—when she greeted him each morning at the factory or saw his smile or bantered with him—that she'd felt a new awareness of Hugh stirring inside her. But she wasn't sure that meant she could feel—*did feel*—anything more than friendship for him.

The idea of marrying again, even for love, sent shards of apprehension through her. Her grief over Ned had faded, though it would likely always be there. However, did that mean she was brave enough to give her heart away a second time, now that she knew the real possibility of losing the one who held it?

"I suppose that is something to ponder," she conceded at last.

Smiling, he tipped his head in the direction of the house. "Give me a chance to redeem myself in another race."

"Of course." She was more than relieved to return their focus to riding.

Hugh spurred his horse forward into a gallop, throwing her a boyish grin over his shoulder. Ada and her horse rushed after them. Thankfully, they'd left the troubling subject of marriage behind.

Still, as she rode toward Whitmore House, she couldn't ignore the unsettled feeling in the pit of her stomach that suggested the topic was not gone and buried. It would eventually come up again.

Chapter 20

April 1918

SHUTTING THE BEDTIME story, Ada pressed a kiss to her daughter's forehead and set the book on the side table. "Time for bed, pet."

"Not yet," Rosemary pouted as she slid beneath her covers. "I'm not sleepy." This was followed by a large yawn that made Ada smile.

She smoothed back Rosemary's hair. "Do you have your doll?"

"Yes." The girl lifted the doll from its spot beside her.

While Victoria had given her granddaughter a great many dolls, her favorite was still the one from Ada's grandmother. Ada suspected that was because the doll looked so much like Rosemary—it was almost like having a sister.

Sadness stole over her at the thought. She would have loved for her daughter to have siblings.

There's still time, her heart whispered. But Ada shook off the notion. She and Rosemary were fine, weren't they, just the two of them?

"What would you like for your birthday, Mummy?" Rosemary asked as Ada moved toward the door and turned off the light.

Ada could hardly believe it would soon be her birthday again. That meant she'd been working as Hugh's secretary for seven months now. The modest income had proven helpful on more than one occasion, especially after she'd sold off a large tract of land last autumn. Most of the money from the sale had gone to fund the drainage project.

While the estate was still in trouble, and the drawn-out war overseas was not helping matters, Ada was hopeful this year's crop would be better. If not . . . She mentally shook her head. The future might be uncertain, but she would not live in fear and doubt as she once had. Through her own experiences of faith and prayer, she knew God was aware of her. And she would do her best to keep trusting Him.

"Mummy?"

Ada laughed. "Sorry, pet. You asked what I want for my birthday." She tapped her chin with her finger. "Let me think."

"I have three pennies. Would you like those? You can use them to help pay for the house. Or you could buy a sweet, and I'd only ask for one bite."

From the light spilling in from the hallway, Ada caught the earnest look on her daughter's face. That, combined with Rosemary's sincere words, elicited a solid lump in her throat and robbed her of the ability to answer for a moment.

An immense feeling of satisfaction washed through her. Just as she and Ned had hoped and dreamed, they'd raised a daughter who was learning compassion, sacrifice, and the value of relationships. And Ada was still doing that while living at Stonefield, as evidenced by Rosemary's tender birthday offering.

"Sweets do sound delicious, Rosie." She walked back to

her daughter's bed. "But what I'd like most for my birthday is something from the heart."

Her daughter's face scrunched in confusion. "Like what?"

"A picture," she said, kneeling down. "Or a letter. Or perhaps a song on the piano."

Rosemary grinned. "Oh, I understand."

"So keep your pennies." She tapped her daughter playfully on the nose, which inspired Rosemary's delightful giggle. "And if you buy a sweet, I only want one bite."

The girl nodded. "Good night, Mummy."

"Good night, pet." She placed a kiss on Rosemary's cheek.

In spite of the challenges she'd faced and the loss of loved ones she'd endured, Ada could honestly say her life was still full. That was something else to ponder and celebrate.

Ada wrapped her sweater tighter around her as she strolled alongside Hugh. He'd asked her to go on a walk after church today. However, it would have to be a short one. Gray clouds scuttled across the sky, promising rain sooner than later.

"Thank you again for coming last night, Hugh."

She had invited him and his mother, along with the O'Reillys and her grandmother, to dine at Stonefield in celebration of her birthday. Her mother had expressed initial embarrassment at hosting, given that their meals were much simpler, their staff much reduced, these days. But everyone who came seemed to enjoy themselves. After a while, even Victoria relaxed.

"It was a delightful evening," he said, throwing her a smile. "Especially the song Rosemary played on the piano."

That had been her daughter's present to her, and Ada had adored it. Minnie had managed to procure enough sugar to make a delicious cake, and Ada's mother and grandmother had both gifted her with pieces of jewelry from their collections.

Hugh apparently had something for her, too. He'd mentioned it Friday at the factory, but said he would wait to give it to her once they had a moment alone.

As if reading her thoughts, he stopped and slipped his hand inside his jacket. "Are you ready for your gift?"

Ada nodded. She'd felt the most anticipation for what his present might be. *Because he's a dear friend,* she told herself. Still, it hadn't escaped her notice how handsome he looked today in his walking suit and hat.

"I hope you like it." He handed her a slip of paper.

She laughed softly in confusion. "What's this?"

"Read it."

Unfolding the paper, she read the scrawled note out loud. "I, Hugh Whittington, bequeath my horse Queen Mary . . ." She shot him a shocked look before he motioned for her to continue. "To Ada Thorne Henley on this, her birthday, the twentieth of April 1918." He'd signed his name below the message.

"You're giving me a . . . a horse?" Not just any horse, either. Queen Mary was the horse she rode whenever they went riding together.

A full smile lifted the corners of his mouth. "It's a bit unconventional, I admit, but I know how much you enjoy riding. The horse can remain at the stables at Whitmore House and is yours to take out whenever you wish, whether I am with you or not."

Ada pressed the note to her heart and rested her other hand on his sleeve. "It's a wonderful gift. Thank you."

On impulse, she rose on tiptoe and pressed a quick kiss to his cheek. The pleasant scent of his shaving soap wafted over her as she lowered herself back to the ground.

"Ada," Hugh murmured. He took her hand in his and regarded her gravely. "There is something else I need to—"

At that moment, the clouds unleashed their rain, spilling it in great drops. Ada kept the paper clutched to her sweater to protect it and looked around for someplace to take shelter. The old oak tree at the edge of the field—where she'd once met Ned—was the only possibility.

"We can shelter under the tree," she said, hurrying in that direction.

She rushed across the field and slipped beneath the splayed branches of the oak. Thankfully, they blocked a good portion of the rain. A second later, Hugh joined her beside the tree's massive trunk.

"So much for a walk." She shook her head ruefully.

Hugh chuckled as he removed his damp hat, his gaze full of warm amusement.

Before she could ask what he'd been about to say, she noticed the lock of brown hair that had fallen onto his forehead. Ada lifted her hand and brushed aside the hair, then let her fingers skim the shadows of his jaw. Her stomach fluttered with delight at the feel of his clean-shaven face beneath her fingertips. But just as quickly, she felt embarrassment at her boldness. What had compelled her to do such a thing?

She had started to lower her arm, her cheeks heating with a fierce blush, when Hugh caught her hand in his. He pressed a kiss to her palm. The feather-light stroke contrasted with the intent focus in his brown eyes and made her heart throb faster.

"Ada," he murmured, his eyes intent on hers. He released her hand and cupped her face.

When his lips sought hers, she wasn't startled or disappointed. His touch was tentative and questioning, yet deliciously wonderful at the same time. It had been ages since she'd last kissed a man, and that had been Ned.

Banishing all thoughts to the back of her mind, Ada threaded her arms around Hugh's neck. He deepened their kiss, and its tenderness strengthened the unevenness of her pulse.

Too soon, he eased back. "There is something I must confess." His thumb trailed her cheek. "It's what I wished to say earlier."

"Yes?" she said, resting her head against his chest.

When he encircled her in his arms, she sighed with contentment. Had she unconsciously hoped for this new turn in their relationship? She couldn't say for certain, but she did know she loved being held by him.

"Are you going to tell me?" She moved just enough to give Hugh an encouraging smile.

There was no lightheartedness in his expression. "Yes, and it is simply this." His next words were spoken quietly, but they rumbled in her ears as loudly as thunder. "I wish to marry you, Ada."

She froze within his embrace. Confusion, and a sliver of dread, kept her from replying.

"For years, I admired you from afar," he continued, his voice beseeching her to understand. "And though I have tried to deny it, those feelings have only grown more pronounced since your return last summer."

Ada stepped back, her fingers rising to her lips. They still tingled from his fervent kiss. Hugh had harbored feelings for her for years?

"But . . . why did you not say something back then?"

He spread his arms in a helpless gesture. "By the time I felt I could, you were already in love with Ned."

A shiver that had less to do with the cold and more to do with her muddled emotions ran through her. She folded her arms against it.

"Is this about saving Stonefield?" She glanced down at the tree roots near their feet, afraid of his answer. Hugh hadn't brought up marriage as a solution to her troubles since last October. "I told you I would not marry for money."

He narrowed the short distance between them and softly nudged her chin upward until she was peering at him again. "This has nothing to do with Stonefield, unless you wish to use my money to help save it." The earnest light in his gaze made her grateful she had the tree trunk at her back for support. "This is about my heart and my deep, resounding love for you."

My deep, resounding love. Those were nearly the same words she'd used last fall in describing the kind of love she'd had with Ned, the kind of love she wanted again if she married a second time. That Hugh had remembered her exact wording brought tears to her eyes.

This time, his kiss was firm and full of hope. "I realize you still mourn Ned, and I respect that," he said, inching back. Ada's heart beat so hard in her chest, she felt certain he could hear it. "But I hope for more than friendship from you. I wish to know you as my wife, and God-willing, as the mother to our own children."

"And if not . . ." Her voice broke.

Hugh caressed her lower lip, his expression one of love and hopefulness but also anguish. Then he straightened and put his hat back on. "If not, I will understand. But I cannot keep living this way. Either deny my proposal and set me free, or accept my hand in marriage."

"May I have some time, to consider everything?" she managed to ask over the tears clogging her throat.

His nod came at once. "You may take tomorrow and Tuesday off from the factory, if you'd like. Then share your answer with me after that."

"Thank you." She was grateful she wouldn't have to pretend at work as if nothing had changed between them, when everything had.

Another thought left her frowning. If she didn't accept his proposal, how would she manage interacting with him at the factory afterward? Perhaps it was time for Hugh to find a new secretary.

The moment he started across the field, she dropped to the moist ground beneath the tree, chilled and troubled. She couldn't imagine her life without Hugh. But could she marry him? Could she risk her heart like that again?

"Please, Lord," she whispered as the first of her tears slid down her cheeks and off her trembling chin. "Help me know what I'm to do."

As he walked away, Hugh did his best not to hang his head in regret or fear. He'd been honest with Ada about his feelings, at long last, and in doing so had rid himself of a great weight.

That he loved her had no longer been a question in his mind for weeks now. Still, he'd been praying and asking God for help with what to do with his realization.

The answer that had come—to share his feelings with her—had been both welcome and frightening. However, he might not have had the courage to voice his thoughts if Ada hadn't unexpectedly touched his face. In that moment, Hugh couldn't have held back his heart from her if he'd wanted, and so he had kissed her. And the splendor of that kiss had bolstered his bravery.

He'd expected her shock and the need for time to contemplate his proposal, but part of him had foolishly hoped she would accept him on the spot. There was the likelihood of her saying no, and he would lose the only woman he'd ever loved—all over again. But he could not keep silent any longer.

"It's in Thy hands now," he murmured, half in thought, half in prayer.

He loved Ada, more deeply now than he ever had in the past, but he wouldn't be praying over the next few days that she'd agree to become his wife. No, Hugh would be praying that whatever her answer, he would have the strength, the courage, and the compassion to accept it.

Chapter 21

THE NEXT MORNING, after seeing Rosemary off to school, Ada walked to her grandmother's. She wasn't entirely sure who she wished to unburden yesterday's events to—Gran or Minnie. She hadn't yet shared Hugh's proposal with her mother, though she hadn't stopped thinking about it, either. It had been the sole thing on her mind the rest of the day and evening, leaving her with little appetite and a night spent tossing and turning.

It wasn't until Gran's modest estate came into view that Ada knew whose advice she needed most. She knocked on the open door of the kitchen, knowing Minnie would be there instead of in her cottage at this hour. "Morning," she said as she entered.

"Miss Ada!" Molly O'Reilly glanced up from the castle she'd constructed out of wooden blocks.

Minnie paused in her work at the large preparation table in the center of the room to smile at Ada, her surprise evident. "What are you doing 'ere this time of day? Aren't you supposed to be at the factory?"

Ada feigned a smile as she shrugged. "I have the day off

and wondered if you and Molly might wish to join me for a walk."

"Everything all right?" Minnie eyed her shrewdly.

She glanced at Molly, who was watching them. "Mostly, yes."

"No need to say more," her friend said with a knowing look. "Let me just get this 'ere bread in the oven, and then you've got us for twenty minutes."

Any time with her oldest and dearest friend would be a boon. "That would be wonderful."

Minnie nodded, then bustled about finishing her tasks while Molly chattered away to Ada. When the bread was in the oven, Minnie removed two hats from the pegs by the door. She put one on Molly and the other on herself. Ada led the way outside.

"Is that the hat you wore to the party?" she asked as she and Minnie traversed the drive. She wasn't quite ready to confess the true reason for her visit, in spite of Molly running ahead, out of earshot.

Minnie smiled and touched her hat brim. "It is. Do you like it?" Ada nodded. "It's new, and Thomas says I look for any excuse to wear it. Even on a little ol' walk." She chuckled. "But 'e's right."

"Have you been happy living here?" She hadn't expected to ask such a question, but she felt a sudden need to know her friend had found contentment in Yorkshire.

Linking her arm through Ada's, Minnie said, "We're quite 'appy. Look at Molly there, runnin' free and safe. My other wee ones will get to do the same when they come 'ome from school today. Thomas and I both bring in steady money." Her husband was employed at the boot factory. "And your gran is a clever and kind woman."

"I'm glad to hear that."

When Ada fell silent, Minnie nudged her in the side.

"What's your real reason for comin' out today? 'Sides askin' about us and seein' my new 'at?" She laughed lightly.

Ada gazed over the fields spreading out on both sides of the country road. "Hugh wishes to marry me," she said without preamble.

Minnie stopped walking, her eyes round with shock. "When did 'e say that?"

"Yesterday on our walk." A fresh wave of confusion buffeted her. "He told me that he had loved me in the past, before I married Ned, and that he still loves me. Only, I believed we were friends. At least until we ..." Her cheeks flushed, and she let her voice trail out.

"Kissed?" Minnie's green eyes sparkled with delight. "Did you enjoy it?"

Ada's blush deepened. "Perhaps." She began walking again. "Very well. Yes. I enjoyed it quite a lot."

Minnie fell into step with her. "Then what's the trouble?"

"I had no plans to marry again." Ada brushed strands of her hair from her face, propelled there by the breeze. Up ahead, Molly paused to wait for them. When they drew closer, she dashed ahead, giggling.

Her friend's expression conveyed empathy. "But now?"

"I care very much for him."

"Do you love 'im, though?"

Ada's shoulders rose and fell in a helpless shrug. "There are moments when I'm certain I do, and others when I'm perfectly content to remain as we are."

"Will things stay that way, if'n you don't choose to marry 'im?" Minnie asked perceptively.

She shook her head, sadness slashing through her once more at the thought of no longer having Hugh's friendship. "He confessed he cannot keep living as friends when he wishes for so much more."

"Can you blame 'im?"

"No." Ada glanced down at her shoes. "But I can't imagine not having him in my life anymore."

"Maybe that's your answer, then."

She kicked at a pebble. "Maybe. What would you do? If Thomas hadn't returned..."

"I can't see myself sharing my life with anyone but 'im," Minnie admitted after a moment. "Especially the 'ard bits. But I don't know as I would want to give up on lovin' another man, either, if Thomas 'adn't come back. We've likely got years ahead of us, Ada. 'Ow do you wish to spend them?"

The question pierced her to the core. How did she wish to spend the remaining years of her life? Alone with Rosemary and her mother at Stonefield Hall if they were able to keep the house? Or with someone who loved her and shared the same deep faith she had?

"I could lose him either way," she blurted out, a shudder running through her. "I don't know if I could bear that."

Her friend left off walking to give her a hug. "We don't know what the future 'olds. But remember all them times in London when we were brave, with'n God's 'elp?"

She nodded against Minnie's shoulder.

"This time's no different." Minnie eased back, her mouth turned up in a comforting smile. "When do you give 'im your answer?"

"The day after tomorrow." Ada brushed at the damp corners of her eyes.

"You'll know what to do. You will."

Minnie's reassurance wrapped itself around Ada like a warm blanket. Speaking with her friend had been the right thing to do.

"Time to turn back, Molly," Minnie called to her daughter. The little girl spun around and raced past them, back the way they'd come. "In the meantime, why don't you 'ave some of my shortbread and a nice cup of tea. Those never 'urt when tryin' to make up one's mind."

Ada smiled. "And if it ruins my appetite for dinner?"

"All the better."

As she and Minnie exchanged a laugh, the burden around her heart felt lighter. She still had two days to decide what to tell Hugh, and she wouldn't stop hoping and praying she'd have her answer by then.

Ada dreamt that night of the oak tree and the suffocating fog—it was the same dream she'd had years ago in Scotland before she and Ned had married. The same anticipation for Ned's arrival filled her, followed by the confusion and fear when he didn't. This time, Ada called out his name, but the sound was swallowed up by the mist.

Bracing herself against the tree's trunk, she hung her head in defeat. Then her ears caught the sound of approaching footsteps. Her heart sped up, and she lifted her chin. She peered through the fog to see who was coming. A tall figure appeared, hurrying through the mist toward her. Immediate relief replaced her worry.

But it wasn't Ned who approached—it was Hugh. Ada felt mild perplexity at this turn of events, yet the sight of Hugh's warm smile and brown eyes was wonderfully familiar. A sense of security and anticipation wound through her as he scooped up her hand in his . . .

She reluctantly woke. Unlike the last time she'd had this dream, she didn't want it to end. The same pleasant feelings of well-being and eagerness she'd felt at seeing Hugh lingered with her. Could the dream itself be her answer?

Yesterday, she'd spent hours walking, thinking, praying. When her energy ran out before her usual work hours at the factory, she finally retraced her steps home. Her mother had been as surprised to see her as Minnie had. Ada had finally shared with her the news of Hugh's proposal. Victoria had been nearly beside herself with excitement over the possibility of her daughter marrying Hugh Whittington.

"Of course, you would have to resign your position as his secretary," she'd stated in a firm tone as she set aside the book she was reading. "But he can save Stonefield Hall, Ada."

"I am aware of that, Mamma, but I will not accept his hand purely for financial gain."

"No one is saying otherwise." Victoria threw her an exasperated look. "You seem to care for him, so agreeing to his proposal would simply be a matter of affection *and* money."

Is that what she wanted Hugh to believe? That she'd married him for love as well as money? "We shall see," she replied noncommittally.

Victoria repeated her arguments twice more that evening, but thankfully not when Rosemary had been present. Ada merely nodded both times. She didn't want to debate the matter further or waste energy trying to help her mother understand things Victoria wouldn't.

Pushing aside yesterday's conversations, she clung to the memory from her dream. Eventually, she drifted back to sleep.

She woke several hours later. The sun had yet to make its appearance for the day. Staring in the direction of the bed's canopy, Ada considered whether to sleep longer or rise, in spite of the early hour. The thought of lying in bed and then fielding her mother's inevitable questions at breakfast sounded far less appealing than an early morning walk. Hopefully, the exercise would help her solidify her thoughts into an answer.

Throwing off her blankets, Ada stood and dressed quickly. She scrawled a note for her mother, letting her and Rosemary know she'd stepped out, then she placed it on the floor outside Victoria's bedroom door.

She opted for a hat and coat instead of her sweater. The morning coolness that filled her lungs and washed over her cheeks made her grateful for the extra warmth. Gravel crunched underfoot as she made her way down the drive. The sun began its rise, touching her and the green world with ever-increasing rays.

Over the last day-and-a-half, Ada had gone back and forth between accepting Hugh's proposal and letting go of his friendship. There were moments when the thought of marrying him put a schoolgirl grin on her face, and others when doubt consumed her. Could she move on without him in her life? And if she couldn't, was she brave enough to give love a second chance?

Perhaps there were other widows in the world who were contemplating this very question at this moment. Ada found the notion comforting—she was likely not alone in wondering if she could risk giving her heart to another man.

Almost unbidden, her feet turned and headed in the direction of the oak tree. The growing light of dawn lit her way as Ada breathed yet another prayer heavenward.

Help me know what to do, Lord. I care deeply for Hugh. But is that enough to go forward and marry him?

How many times had she trod this footpath on her way to meet Ned? Too many to count. It wasn't hard to conjure up the same giddy feeling in her stomach that she'd had each time she made this walk, knowing who would be waiting for her at the end. Unbeknownst to her, though, another good man had been watching and waiting for her as well.

A sudden thought struck her. If she'd come to care for

Hugh back then and had married him, she never would have left Yorkshire. She wouldn't have known such wonderful years with Ned and Rosemary. Or met Minnie and her family. Or found herself in London and grown a deep, abiding faith.

She was meant to marry Ned when she did.

And what if Hugh had married in her absence? The possibility bothered her, bringing with it a tremor of jealousy. If he'd married, Ada would've been bereft of a close friend, someone she could wholly confide in and trust.

"It's more than that, though," she chided out loud.

She recalled their open, honest conversations, their bantering, their horse rides. It wasn't difficult for her to remember how right and wonderful it had felt to be in Hugh's arms the day of her father's funeral, and again during their kiss by the oak tree. Something deep within her, something stronger than friendship, now stirred inside her each time she interacted with him.

Could that be love?

The prospect brought her up short. She hurried to a nearby stile and lowered herself onto the bottom step.

Recognizing her love for Ned had been easy because it had come almost immediately—like a burst of light in a cold world. In contrast, her feelings for Hugh had grown gradually, like the sun's morning rays, beginning with their letters and blossoming from there. Yet that didn't mean those feelings were any less real or bright—or any less rooted in a deep, resounding love.

"I love him," she whispered. "I do. I love him." The relief and gratitude she felt at finally having an answer spilled out of her in the form of a laugh.

However, her mother's words from the day before returned to her mind and intruded upon her joy. She loved Hugh, yes, and his money would certainly help save the estate.

But would one or both of them wonder someday which had been Ada's true motive for marrying him? She didn't want him doubting her love or her answer.

If it came down to having Stonefield or Hugh, she knew exactly which one she would choose—every time.

"Which is precisely what I must tell him." Ada looked out across the nearby field. She didn't want to wait until tomorrow to give Hugh her answer, not when she knew her mind and heart now.

Resolved, she climbed the stile and struck out across the field. The temperature remained cool and hinted at rain, despite the intermittent sunshine. Still, she didn't want to walk back to Stonefield to catch a ride in their automobile. If she hurried to the factory on foot, she would likely get there before Hugh did, then she could surprise him with her news.

She hardly noticed the countryside as she strolled purposefully across it. Soon, the rain began to fall, but her damp clothes and stockings couldn't alter her spirits.

However, by the time the factory came into view, Ada was shivering and wet. She had no idea how long the walk had taken, but she saw Mr. Nelson, the foreman, striding toward the factory entrance. Was Hugh already there, too?

"Mr. Nelson!" she called, increasing her pace.

The man turned, his eyebrows hiking up. "Mrs. Henley? You're a wee bit earlier than normal, aye?"

"I have some business that needs tending to first thing."

Mr. Nelson nodded.

"Is Mr. Whittington here?" She held her breath, realizing she didn't know exactly what time Hugh typically arrived.

The foreman, thankfully, shook his head. "I doubt it. He'll be along by seven, for certain, but he rarely arrives before that."

Ada exhaled with relief as Mr. Nelson unlocked the door

and let her inside. She made her way to her desk and was delighted to see that Hugh's office still sat dark and empty.

After turning on the light, she removed her hat and set it on one of the chairs to dry. She rubbed her chilled hands together to warm them as she wandered the room. She'd been inside Hugh's office countless times since coming to work for him, but today, she saw his things with new eyes. The eyes of a woman in love.

She smiled to herself as she took a seat behind his desk. Her toes tapped out an impatient rhythm against the wood floor as she waited for his arrival. Soon, the tread of footfalls floated through the open door—much like in her dream. Ada's heart beat double time beneath her dress.

Clearly lost in thought, Hugh didn't notice her right away, which gave her a chance to study him unawares through the open doorway. Weary determination radiated from him as he hung up his hat and coat and propped his umbrella against the outer wall of the office. The tired lines of his handsome face begged her to smooth them away. Perhaps her answer would.

He entered the room and stopped short when his gaze met hers. "Ada? What are you doing here?"

"Hello." She rose to her feet, her pulse careening recklessly again. "I didn't know if I would arrive before you." She laughed nervously. "It was a longer walk than I expected."

He blinked in surprise. "You . . . you walked all the way to the factory? This morning?"

"Yes, I needed to speak with you." She circled his desk and stopped a few feet from him.

Hugh frowned slightly. "Is something the matter?"

"No, no." An unexpected shyness crept over her, binding her tongue. "It's just . . ."

His brow furrowed with confusion, but he smiled

patiently. "Must be rather important for you to come all this way in the rain."

How she loved his smile and humor—and everything that was him.

Ada studied his face and found herself staring at his masculine lips. The memory of their kiss filled her thoughts. She wanted to kiss him again, right now, and every day after.

Gathering her courage, she marched up to him, took his beloved face between her hands, and pressed a firm kiss to his mouth. Hugh hesitated only a moment before wrapping his arm around her and cupping the back of her neck with his free hand. The closeness of him, along with the rapid strumming of her heartbeat, warmed her completely.

She eased back after a long minute, though she stayed within his half-embrace. "I love you, Hugh Whittington, and I wish to marry you."

"Truly?" When she nodded, he bent toward her, intent on another kiss.

Ada pressed her finger to his lips. "I do have two stipulations."

"Should I be worried?" he asked in a playful tone after kissing her fingertip.

Smiling fully, she shook her head. "Not in the least."

"Very well. What are these stipulations?"

Hopefully, he would understand and agree with them. "First, I would like to continue working as your secretary, without wages. I love the work, but more importantly, I love the man I work with."

"I have no qualms with that," he said, grinning. "Saves me the trouble of replacing the best secretary I have had to date." He sneaked a quick kiss in before asking, "And the second stipulation?"

Ada drew in a deep breath and let it out slowly. "We will

need to live at Whitmore House. Because I am going to sell Stonefield Hall."

"Sell?" Hugh's eyebrows rose. "I can restore the estate."

She placed her hand alongside his jaw, and Hugh leaned into her touch. "You could, but I don't wish for you to ever question that I married you for any reason other than my deep love for you."

His gaze searched hers, then, apparently seeing her earnestness, he dipped his head in a nod. "If you're certain, I will agree to that stipulation as well."

"I am."

He clasped her hands in his and drew her closer. "None of this could wait until tonight or tomorrow?"

"No, not after I'd figured out my own heart." She laughed self-consciously. "So rain or shine, I had to come."

The slow smile he gave her made her stomach tumble with anticipation. "I believe that is nearly as wonderful to hear as your answer."

His lips sought hers again, the promise of the future in his touch. Ada wished to linger in the moment forever. She could hardly believe that less than an hour ago, she'd been sitting on that stile, wondering what her answer ought to be. Now it throbbed, true and firm, inside her. God had given her—given them—a second chance at love, and she would do her best to never take that for granted.

"I love you," Hugh said when their kiss ended. "And I pledge to love you every day of my life."

Tears of happiness and hope filled her eyes. "I'm praying that will be full of many, many more days."

"As do I, my love." He brushed away a tear that escaped her lashes. "But whether many or few, we can welcome every day that we have."

He rested her hands against his chest, where she could

feel the swift beating of his heart in tandem with her own. His contemplative expression made her wonder if he, too, was thinking of Ned and Harry. "Agreed?" he asked.

"Agreed," she repeated before kissing him once more.

Epilogue

August 1919

"Look here, miss," the man with the camera called to Rosemary.

Ada gently squeezed her oldest daughter's hand. "Keep your eyes on the camera, pet." When Rosemary complied, Ada moved closer to Hugh, his arm wrapped snugly around her shoulders. His other hand rested on the perambulator, where their three-month-old daughter, Amelia Jane, slept soundly, oblivious to the goings-on above her.

"Now, everybody, look this way." The photographer held the roll film camera with its black bellows at his waist. "Very nice. The house in the background looks quite lovely."

A mixture of sadness and pride filled Ada at his words. Tomorrow, Stonefield Hall would pass to a new owner. It had taken her and Hugh more than a year to find a willing buyer, but at last, a man of means from York had seen the beauty and potential of the estate and had offered to buy it.

Ada had been trying to think of some way to honor her childhood home and preserve its memories for her daughters.

She had some knickknacks, a few pieces of furniture, and a modest number of paintings she'd brought to Whitmore House after she and Hugh had married. But she had no visual reminders of what the estate itself had looked like. Hugh's suggestion to take a photograph in front of the red-brick house had been perfect and timely.

The photographer lifted his chin long enough to shoot them a smile. "Here we go." He clicked the camera once, twice, three times. Ada soon lost track of the number.

"How much longer, Mummy?" Rosemary whispered from the corner of her mouth. "My lips hurt."

Ada's laughter was matched by Hugh's as the camera clicked some more. After another minute or two, the photographer announced they were finished. Rosemary ran across the lawn to where Helena stood waiting for them.

A feeling of sadness washed over Ada at the thought that her mother, who had passed away during last fall's influenza epidemic, wasn't here to join them in the photograph today. She missed both her parents. The three of them might have disagreed on many things, especially her and her mother over the sale of the estate. Victoria had been angry at Ada for weeks. Eventually, though, she'd come to see Ada's decision for what it was, in large part with help from Helena. After that, Ada and her mother had developed a much closer relationship that had continued until Victoria's passing.

"I'll have the film developed this week, Mr. Whittington," the photographer said.

Hugh nodded. "Thank you. Baxter will drive us back to Whitmore House."

"Give me a moment." Ada touched Hugh's arm.

He placed his hand on top of hers. "Saying goodbye?"

"Yes," she whispered from her suddenly tight throat.

"I'll assist Mamma and the girls into the car."

Thanking him, she walked back toward the house, tilting her chin to gaze at the familiar walls and windows. She'd lived most of her life here, save for seven years in London and the last fifteen months at Whitmore House. Tears blurred her view of the red brick.

Today, she wasn't just saying goodbye to Stonefield Hall. In many ways, she was saying goodbye once again to her parents and to her childhood.

Ada sensed more than heard Hugh approach from behind, then felt his hands rest reassuringly on her shoulders. "So many, many memories," she said in a tear-choked voice.

"To be sure." He pressed a light kiss to her hair. "Are you certain you wish to sell it? You can still change your mind."

She turned to face him, love enveloping her sadness. "If you mean do I regret choosing you over the house ..." Ada pressed a firm kiss to his mouth, not caring that the photographer, the chauffeur, and their family looked on. "Then the answer is, and always will be, never, Hugh Whittington—no matter how many memories this place holds for me."

"A fact I cherish every day," he murmured, his brown eyes full of tenderness. "I love you, Ada."

"I love you."

Her life had turned out far differently than she'd expected when she had walked down this same drive nine years ago. She had loved, and lost, and loved again. And through it all, she'd discovered a strength and courage inside herself that she hadn't known she possessed. She had learned about faith, too, and what it really meant to experience God's loving care, especially during the most difficult days of her life.

Gazing at the house one last time, she drew in a deep breath and released it. "I'm ready," she said as she slipped her hand into Hugh's.

There would likely be difficult days ahead, ones filled

with some measure of loss like today, and others that required good courage. She supposed that was true of any life lived to its fullest. But as Hugh smiled tenderly at her, she also knew there were many bright and beautiful days in store for them, too.

Author's Note

During a research trip to England in 2013, I visited the Imperial War Museum in Manchester. While there, I purchased a fantastic little book called *First World War Britain* by Peter Doyle. I researched much about World War One for my *Of Love and War* series, but there were details in Doyle's book that I hadn't known. I wrote Ada's story, in part, to share these fascinating details of life in England during the First World War.

The flat in London where Ada lives is based on one from the Latchmere Estate housing project in Battersea. Concerned about the living conditions of the working man, a number of politicians oversaw the building of houses and flats that were far better than the city's overcrowded, dismal slums. The houses and flats in the Latchmere Estate each had a bath scullery, a boiler and range, and electric lighting.

The bank holiday of August 1914 was four days long. Greatly concerned about a financial panic in the wake of Britain declaring war on Germany that same week, the government extended the regular one-day holiday to four—and successfully averted any disaster. People were actually depositing money the day after the holiday instead of withdrawing it, as had been feared.

After Belgian refugees arrived in London in October 1914, there were a number of German butcher shops and bakeries that were looted. This was only a portent of things to come. With the sinking of the RMS *Lusitania* in May 1915, there was even greater rioting and violence against Germans in London.

Like Ada, there were women who worked during the war to help recycle old paper. I found this detail while looking through some intriguing pictures in a *Daily Mail* article that highlighted different jobs women were employed in during the war. In one picture, women were taking apart giant railway ledgers, and in another, they were standing atop massive piles of paper and sorting through them.

When we normally think of London being bombed, scenes of World War Two come to mind, but the city was also bombed during the First World War—by zeppelins at first, and later, German airplanes. During one such bombing, a bomb did, in fact, hit a school in Poplar, East London. Eighteen children were killed, most of whom were younger than six years old. A collection was taken up to help provide the grieving mothers and their surviving children with a two-week holiday in Berkshire.

Prior to World War One, secretarial jobs weren't typically filled by women. However, like many aspects of life during this time, the war would open up careers to women that had once been largely filled by men.

Stonefield Hall and Whitmore House are both my fictional creations, as is the boot factory. There is a factory in Wales, still in operation today, that made boots for Australian soldiers during both world wars.

Britain has long held a fascination for me. My hope is that through Ada's story, readers will get a real sense of the country's beauty and what life was like during this interesting time in its history.

A *USA Today* bestselling author, Stacy Henrie graduated from Brigham Young University with a degree in public relations. Not long after, she switched from writing press releases and newsletters to writing inspirational historical romances. Born and raised in the West, where she currently resides with her family, she enjoys reading, road trips, interior decorating, chocolate, and most of all, laughing with her husband and kids. Her books include *Hope at Dawn*, a 2015 RITA Award finalist for excellence in romance. You can learn more about Stacy and her books by visiting her website: StacyHenrie.com.

www.ingramcontent.com/pod-product-compliance
Lightning Source LLC
LaVergne TN
LVHW021810060526
838201LV00058B/3308